'Elijah, what on—?'

She never got to finish, never got to say another word, because his mouth was on hers, his flesh pressing hers, his skin warm against her frozen cheeks. He pinned her against the wall, kissing her cheeks, her eyes, as he took her icy hands. Then, just as she regrouped, just as she opened her mouth to speak, his lips hushed her again. She could feel him pressing a ring on her finger.

The whole intoxicating, dizzying contact took seconds, perhaps, but it utterly, utterly spun her mind. This kiss was nothing like the one they had shared last night.

She pushed him back, frightened by his fervour, till her eyes met his. She frowned at the silent plea she saw there... Another presence was making itself known—a figure on the peripheries of her vision, walking down the hall.

'Ms Anderson!' Elijah's hand gripped hers tightly. 'This is Ainslie...'

'Ainslie?'

The middle-aged woman was picking up Guido. Maybe she was an aunt Elijah had discovered? Maybe the relatives had arrived and they were talking? Or a neighbour, perhaps? All these thoughts whirred through her head as a very dishevelled and bemused Ainslie offered her hand.

'Is this the nanny?'

'The nanny?' Elijah let out a slightly incredulous laugh. 'Heavens, no—didn't I tell you? Ainslie is my fiancée.'

Carol Marinelli recently filled in a form where she was asked for her job title and was thrilled, after all these years, to be able to put down her answer as writer. Then it asked what Carol did for relaxation, and after chewing her pen for a moment Carol put down the truth: writing. The third question asked—What are your hobbies? Well, not wanting to look obsessed or, worse still, boring, she crossed the fingers on her free hand and answered swimming and tennis. But, given that the chlorine in the pool does terrible things to her highlights, and the closest she's got to a tennis racket in the last couple of years is watching the Australian Open—I'm sure you can guess the real answer!

**Carol also writes for Medical™ Romance.
Her latest Medical,
ONE MAGICAL CHRISTMAS,
is out next month!**

HIRED: THE ITALIAN'S CONVENIENT MISTRESS

BY
CAROL MARINELLI

MILLS & BOON®
Pure reading pleasure™

All the characters in this book have no existence outside the imagination of the author, and have no relation whatsoever to anyone bearing the same name or names. They are not even distantly inspired by any individual known or unknown to the author, and all the incidents are pure invention.

First published in Great Britain 2008
Harlequin Mills & Boon Limited,
Eton House, 18-24 Paradise Road, Richmond, Surrey TW9 1SR

© Carol Marinelli 2008

ISBN: 978 0 263 86477 9

Set in Times Roman 10½ on 12¾ pt
01-1108-46925

Printed and bound in Spain
by Litografia Rosés, S.A., Barcelona

HIRED: THE ITALIAN'S CONVENIENT MISTRESS

CHAPTER ONE

WHERE?

Jammed closely between rush hour commuters, her backpack hopefully still by the door where she'd left it, Ainslie didn't even need to hold the handrail to stay standing as the London Underground jolted her towards a destination unknown and her mind begged the question: where could she go?

There was Earls Court, of course—wasn't that where all Australian backpackers went when they were in London?

Only she wasn't backpacking. She had come to London to work. She'd had a job and accommodation already secured, and had been enjoying her work and life for three very full months—until today.

Her thick blonde hair was still dripping from the rain shower she'd been caught in, and beads of sweat broke out onto her brow as another surge of panic hit.

What on earth was she going to do?

Oh, she had friends, of course. Or rather other nannies she'd first met at playgroup, then at weekly get-togethers with the children. Later, on their time off, they'd discovered together all that London had to offer.

Friends who right now would be sitting in a bar. Sitting and listening, aghast, to the news that Ainslie had been fired, had been accused of stealing from her employers. And whether they believed she'd done it or not didn't really matter—their bosses moved in her ex-boss's circles, and if they wanted to keep their jobs the last thing they needed was a branded thief arriving homeless at their doors.

'*Scusi.*' A low male voice growled in her ear as the tube lurched, and the baby the man was holding was pressed further against her.

'It's okay,' Ainslie said, not even looking up, instead trying to move back a touch as the tube halted in a tunnel between stations. But there was no room to manoeuvre, and she arched her back, trying hard not to disturb the sleeping child in his arms.

God, it was hot!

Despite the cold December conditions outside, here on the tube it was boiling. Hundreds of people were crammed together, dressed in winter coats and scarves, damp from the rain, turning the carriage into an uncomfortable sauna, and Ainslie took a grateful gulp of air as someone opened an air vent.

The baby looked hot too. Bundled into a coat, he was wearing gloves and a woolly hat with earflaps—like an old-fashion fighter pilot—and his little cheeks were red and angry. But he didn't seem distressed. In fact he was asleep, long black eyelashes fanning the red cheeks.

Cute kid, Ainslie thought for about a tenth of a second— before her eyes pooled with tears at the thought of Jack and Clemmie, the little charges she hadn't even been allowed to say goodbye to.

'Sorry!' It was now Ainslie's turn to apologise, as she was pushed further against the baby. She saw his little face screw up in discomfort, and she pressed herself back, to try and give him more room, looking up at his father to briefly express her helplessness. Only suddenly she was just that...

Helpless.

Lost, just lost for a moment, as she stared into the most exquisite face she had ever witnessed close up. Glassy blue eyes that were bloodshot briefly met hers. His thick glossy black hair was unkempt, and his black eyelashes were as long as his son's. His mouth was set in a grim line as he nodded his understanding that it wasn't her fault, before his eyes flicked away down to his son, trying to soothe the now restless, grizzling baby back to sleep, talking to him in Italian. But his rich, deep voice did nothing to soothe the child. The babe's eyes fluttered open, as blue as his father's, but it was as if the child didn't even recognise him. His wail of distress caused a few heads to turn.

'Hush, Guido, it is okay...' He was speaking to him in English now—English that was laced with a rich accent as he again attempted to calm the baby. Now that he wasn't looking at her, Ainslie could look at him more closely. Though stunning, he was clearly exhausted, his skin pale, huge violet smudges beneath his eyes, and he needed to shave. The stubble on his jaw was so black it appeared blue.

'Guido, it is okay...' His voice was louder now, as the tube lurched back into motion, but it only distressed the baby further. His back arching like a cat trying to escape, he clawed his way up his father's chest, flinging himself backwards. But there was nowhere to go, and his little face pressed into Ainslie's as his father struggled to contain him.

'It's okay…' Ainslie didn't know if she was talking to the father or his child as he apologised, gained control and pulled the babe tightly in. But Ainslie could see the child's panic, had felt his burning cheek against hers for just a fraction of time—it had been boiling. Instinctively, as if at work, she put her hand to his head and felt him burning beneath it.

'He's hot…' For a second time she looked into the man's eyes, only this time her mind was on the child. 'He has a fever…'

'He's sick…' The man nodded, and Ainslie didn't know if he would have elaborated further because just then the tube pulled into a station, and as commuters piled off and piled on they were separated.

She should have put it out of her mind. Heaven knows she had enough to think about at the moment—like finding somewhere to stay for tonight, finding a job with no reference, clearing her name, telling her mum—only she couldn't. The little boy's screams, though muffled, still reached her; the look on his father's face, the wretched exhaustion, his voice, his eyes, stayed with her. This stranger had whirred her senses. He was wearing a heavy grey coat, but she'd caught a glimpse of a collar and suit. Maybe he'd picked the little boy up from daycare? Perhaps they'd just come from the doctor's…?

What did it matter? Ainslie told herself as the tube pulled into Earls Court station.

According to her guide it was *the* descending place for Australians in London—now all she had to do was find a youth hostel. Pushing her way through the slowly moving masses, relieved that her backpack had amazingly still been where she'd left it, Ainslie stood on the platform, taking a deep breath, glad to be out of the stifling crowd.

She could hear her mobile trilling and sat on a little bench, nervous when she saw that it was Angus, her old boss, calling. Wondering what he had to say, she let the call go through to her message bank, grateful she wouldn't have to come up with an instant answer to any difficult questions he might pose.

Angus Maitlin might be a famous celebrity doctor—one who appeared regularly in magazines and on television—but he was also a consultant in Accident and Emergency and a wise and shrewd man. Living with him for three months, Ainslie had worked that out quickly, and in the evenings when he had been at home, listening to him as he read a book to one of the kids, half watching the evening news Angus had always made her smile.

'There's more to it!' he'd often say at the end of a report—or, 'He did it!' as an emotional plea was read out.

But the memory wasn't making her smile now, as Ainslie wondered how she could possibly lie and get away with it to this wise, shrewd, and also terribly kind man.

'Ainslie—it's Angus. Gemma just told me what happened. I don't know what to say. Look—I don't like that you're out there with no money or references—I hope you're at a friend's. If you needed money…we could have sorted something out. I'm working till late, but I'll ring tomorrow…'

Clearly Angus was finding the situation difficult, because his voice trailed off then, and Ainslie felt tears tumble out of her eyes for the first time since it had happened. Sadly she realised that he believed her to be guilty. She could hear the disappointment in his kind voice.

Well, of course he believed Gemma—she was his wife! A wife who had told her husband that things had been going missing since Ainslie had started. A wife who had told him she had caught the nanny red-handed, having found her ring and necklace in Ainslie's bedroom drawer. Better that than admitting that it was the nanny who had actually caught *her* red-handed.

Or rather red-faced, beneath her lover, when Ainslie had brought the children home unexpectedly early.

Slumped against the wall on the busy platform, Ainslie began crying her eyes out—not loud tears, just shivering gulps as she gave in and wept. She'd been counting on her Christmas bonus—had needed the money desperately, thanks to Nick and the mess that was unfolding back home. It was the first time she'd actually cried since she'd picked up her mail two weeks ago and found out that her ex-boyfriend had, unbeknownst to her, taken out a joint loan while they were together. The deceit had been almost more upsetting than the financial ramifications, and the tears she had held back spilled out now, as she faced the bleakest of Christmases. Not that anyone noticed. Not that anyone even gave her a second glance. Surrounded by people in one of the busiest cities in the world, never had Ainslie felt more alone.

She could hear the baby crying again too, and his loud sobs matched how she felt…

Guido.

The fraught cries snapped Ainslie out of her own introspection, her eyes scanning the platform until she found him.

He wasn't a baby, more a toddler—eighteen months old, perhaps. He was standing—no, sitting. No, now he was lying on the platform floor and kicking his legs, throwing a spectacular tantrum. His less than impressed father was half kneeling, a laptop and briefcase discarded on the platform beside him, holding his child with one hand as with the other he attempted to open a pushchair with all the skill of someone who'd never opened a push-chair in his life—and certainly not while trying to hold onto a frantic toddler.

And just as the crowd had ignored her tears, so too did they ignore this man's plight. Heads down, they just hurried past, and either didn't see or pretended not to notice; everyone was too busy to offer help.

Wiping her cheeks with the back of her hand, Ainslie walked over. 'Can I help?'

She watched him stiffen momentarily. His head was almost automatically shaking in refusal, highlighting that this was clearly a man who wasn't used to accepting help. Then in almost the same instant he let out a reluctant breath and conceded, picking up the little boy and standing to his impressive height.

'Can you open this pushchair?'

'Of course.'

'Please,' he added as a very late afterthought, as with two easy motions Ainslie did just that.

'Thank you.' He dismissed her then, and really she should have turned and gone. But Ainslie knew that an open pushchair was only half the battle. She watched and wondered with vague amusement how he'd manage to get this stiff, angry child into the chair.

With great difficulty he tried to buckle Guido in. Failing on the first effort, he undid his coat, and Ainslie was treated to a glimpse of impressive suit, a shirt unbuttoned at the neck. Even Ainslie could tell that suits and coats as exquisite as the one this man was wearing didn't often belong to a daddy who spent a lot of time at home.

This daddy, Ainslie guessed as Guido's shrieks trebled, must have spent so much time in the office that his son hardly recognised him. There were no easy motions, no practised ease, as he tried to get the unwilling, resisting arms of the child into the straps of the pushchair.

'I can manage!' he growled as she hovered.

But he couldn't. The angry little bundle continued kicking and thumping.

Just as Ainslie had decided to let him do just that and deal with her own problems, Guido caught them both by surprise…

Staring at his father, his screams stopped for a second, a second that allowed him to draw breath, and Ainslie stood open mouthed as the little boy, very deliberately, very angrily and very directly, spat in the face of his father.

'Puh!'

It was no accident—he even added sound—and Ainslie's eyes widened in horror, staring at the shocked expression of the man, who didn't look as if he'd take too well to being spat on. Then he did the most unexpected thing and grinned; that crabby, exhausted, haughty face was actually breaking into a laugh, and it caught the little boy by surprise, because he relaxed just long enough for the pushchair strap to be clicked into place.

The man stood up and, still grinning, pulled out a very smart navy silk handkerchief and wiped his face.

'Little gypsy tramp—just like his father!'

Which wasn't the best of introductions!

'Oh…' Ainslie nodded.

The last remnants of his smile were fading, and, after wrapping the child in a blanket, he took off his coat and wrapped that around the little boy too. But even though it was freezing outside, it was way, way too much for a little boy who was boiling up.

Ainslie couldn't help herself. 'He has a fever!'

'So I keep him warm.'

'No…' Ainslie shook her head in exasperation. 'I work with children, and what he needs is to cool down…' She looked at his bemused expression and knew he didn't have a clue. 'He's *very* hot.' When still he didn't seem to understand, she spoke more loudly, more slowly. 'He might fit…have a convulsion…' she explained.

'I am neither deaf nor stupid! You do not have to speak pigeon English.'

'Sorry…' Ainslie blushed.

'I have just seen a doctor with him, and he has been prescribed some medicine.' He pulled a rather scruffy bag from his pocket, along with a rolled-up tie. 'When I get him home I will give it.'

'But they're antibiotics—what he needs…' Oh, what was the point? Turning on her heel, she gave a shrug. The sooner this arrogant know it all got home to his wife the sooner his boiling, ill-mannered baby could get some paracetamol in him and hopefully cool down.

'He needs what?'

A hand grabbed her arm, and Ainslie felt her throat tighten. He had just *sooo* done the wrong thing. Only he didn't let go, and even though she had a jacket on the inappropriate touch burned through the thick material, just a trickle of fear invading. But she was on a busy tube station, Ainslie reminded herself, and turned around to confront him.

'What is it he needs?'

'Could you remove your hand?' Angry green eyes met his, watched as he blinked and stared down at his hand as if it didn't even belong to him.

'I am sorry!' Instantly he let go—his apology absolutely genuine. 'I am worried about him—and I don't know what to do.'

'Get him home…' Ainslie's voice was softer. 'He needs some paracetamol. Once he's had that he'll settle…'

'Paracetamol?' He checked, and Ainslie nodded.

'And he needs his mum.'

This time she really was going. This time she knew he wouldn't grab her. Only he didn't have to. His voice stilled her as she started walking, his words halting her before she disappeared for ever into the heavy crowd.

'She died this afternoon.'

CHAPTER TWO

His words seared into her. Aghast, she swung around, looked from father to son and back to the father, at the identical blue eyes that stared back at her.

And it was horrible.

That no one knew. That all those strangers had stood on that tube, had tutted at the baby, at the pushchair, had walked past as he'd struggled on the platform—and not a single one knew the misery that was taking place.

There were just a few days until Christmas.

The date didn't matter—it would have been terrible on any day—but that it was so close to Christmas, that this beautiful little boy would be without his mother, that she would be without him, just made it worse somehow. And it made her own problems pale in comparison.

'Can you help me?' His voice was low but there was a thread of urgency.

'Me?'

'You said you work with children?'

'I do, but—'

'Then you must know how to stop his fever? How to take care of him?' There was a plea in his rich voice, a tinge of fear, even panic for his son. 'I don't know what to do. I do not know children; I do not know what this boy needs…' He dived out of his own hell just enough to glimpse her confusion, just long enough to interpret it. 'He is not my son—he is my nephew. There was a car accident. I came from Italy this morning as soon as I hear the news.'

Heard the news. Ainslie opened her mouth to correct him, and then stopped herself—working with people who were usually under three feet tall gave her a tendency to do that! His story certainly explained his visible exhaustion. Dressed in a suit, juggling a laptop and a briefcase along with the stroller, he must have literally left in the middle of whatever it was he was doing and stepped onto a plane.

'Where's his father?' The platform was full—again they were being pushed closer. Only this time they *were* together, sharing this appalling conversation.

Her eyes closed for a second as he answered, 'He died instantly.'

When Ainslie opened them again, he was waiting for her, strong but desperate. His eyes held hers.

'Can you tell me what he needs…help me with him?'

You don't read out a list of questions when you witness someone drowning.

You don't ask their name or age, or if they're worthy of saving. You don't ring for references or ask for a police check—instead you do what you can.

'Yes,' she said simply, because to Ainslie it was just impossible to even think of walking away, of not helping someone who so clearly needed it.

'His home is close by—there is a pharmacy on the way.'

The platform was packed now. Another tube was pulling

in and spewing out its contents. People walked fast as they left the platform, and the station was a blizzard of people, rushing to get home or to go out, stopping to buy their paper, chatting into their phones, arranging dates, parties, meetings—getting on with living.

Getting on with life.

A blast of icy December air hit them as they stepped out onto the busy street. It was the strangest walk; he took her backpack and Ainslie pushed the stroller. Christmas was everywhere—the shops ablaze with decorations, people tipsy from pre-dinner drinks heading for a work party— and it just seemed to magnify his loss. Even the chemist was full of cheery, piped music, chiming Christmas songs, and lazy shoppers were grabbing easy gifts as they stopped to buy Guido's paracetamol.

'Should we get nappies, wipes…or do you have plenty?'

'I haven't been to the house since I arrived—I have no idea what my sister would have. We'd better get them— get whatever you think he might need.'

So she did—put whatever she thought might be needed into a basket and stood trying to hush the little boy as his uncle paid, watching the checkout assistant chatting happily away to her colleague, briefly asking the man if he had had a good day, not noticing that he didn't respond, his face a quilt of muscles as he handed over his credit card.

'I don't know your name.' It was the first thing she said as he made his way back to them.

'Elijah…' He gave a tight smile. 'Elijah Vanaldi. And you?'

'Ainslie Farrell.'

And that was all they said. They walked along in silence

till they came to a quieter street and stopped outside a vast four-storey residence.

But somehow, for now, it was enough.

It was surreal—Elijah working out keys as she stared at the wreath on the door, stepping into someone's house, someone's life, someone you didn't even know, and being entrusted to take care of their most treasured possession. And though it was a beautiful towering white stucco home, as she stepped in, walked along polished floorboards and glimpsed the vast lounge, though her eyes took in the high ceilings and vast windows and expensive furnishings, they didn't merit a mention. The only thing Ainslie could really notice was the collection of shoes and coats in the hall, the scent of pine in the air from the Christmas tree, and the half-cup of cold tea on the granite bench when she walked into the luxury kitchen. Sadness engulfed her when she saw the simple shopping list on the fridge and the breakfast dishes piled by the sink.

Elijah undressed an exhausted Guido.

'Has he had dinner?'

'He had some biscuits, he doesn't seem very hungry.' Elijah held his hand to his forehead. 'He still feels hot. Should I bathe him?'

'I wouldn't worry about it tonight. Let's just get him changed for bed and give him his medicine.' As she wandered upstairs to find pyjamas for Guido, Ainslie could tell that this elegant house with its lavish furniture and expensive fittings was first and foremost a home—a home with a book by the unmade bed, and hair staighteners still plugged in. In the bathroom a tap drizzled, and piles of damp towels and knickers littered the floor, reminding Ainslie that this was a family home that had been left with every intention of coming back.

'She rang me last week to say she was giving in and finally going to get a housekeeper…' His voice behind her made Ainslie jump, and she felt the sting of tears behind her eyes as he walked over and turned off the tap. 'She was never very good at tidying up.'

'Mess doesn't matter.'

'She'd die if she knew we'd seen it like this…' Elijah halted, grimacing at his own words. 'You always had to ring Maria to warn her you coming over—she hated it when people dropped in. She'd hate that she didn't do one of her infamous quick tidies—she'd be embarrassed at someone seeing the place like this.'

'She thought she was coming home.'

'He has an ear infection.' Elijah watched as she easily measured out the antibiotics. 'The doctor said that was why he was miserable and so naughty, but—as I explained to him—from what my sister tells me, and what I have seen of him, he is always trouble!'

'He's got croup too,' Ainslie said, as Guido suitably barked. 'Poor little thing. The medicine should help his pain, though, and the antibiotics will hopefully kick in soon.'

'Hopefully.' Elijah sighed. 'For now I will make him some food, then he can go to bed.' He pulled a piece of paper out of his pocket and looked at it for a moment, then headed to where Guido was sitting on the couch, his eyes half closed, half watching the cartoon that Elijah had put on for him.

There were people who had no idea about children, and people who had *no* idea about children, and Ainslie watched as he peeled a rather overripe banana and handed it to the little boy, who just blinked back at him, bemused.

'Maria said he liked bananas.'

'He's not a monkey…' Ainslie's grin faded. 'Let me,' she said instead, and headed to the kitchen. She found some bread in the freezer and gave it a spin in the microwave, then took off the crusts and put some mashed banana in. She arranged it on a plastic plate and offered it to Guido, who this time accepted it.

Later—when he was falling asleep with exhaustion— Elijah carried his nephew upstairs and Ainslie followed, tucking the little boy, unresisting, into bed.

'He has a night light.' Elijah was looking at his bit of paper again. 'He wakes up, but all he wants is his blanket put back on.'

Watching his strong hands tuck the blanket around the little boy's shoulders, Ainslie could feel her nose running, and had to turn her head quickly away as he straightened up. She headed down the stairs and into the lounge, sniffing away tears as a short time later he came back in, holding two mugs of coffee.

'Thank you.' He handed one to her and sat down, took a sip of his drink and held it in his mouth before talking again. 'I am not a stupid person…'

'I know.' Ainslie gulped. 'I'm sorry about what I said about the banana thing…' She managed a little smile, and he did the same.

'I have nothing, *nothing* to do with children. Nothing!' he added again, in case she hadn't heard it the first or second time. 'And my sister said that she wanted me to have him. That she wanted me to be the one who raises him.'

'What happened?'

For the first time it seemed right to ask—right that she should know a little bit more.

'There was a car accident—it ran off the road and caught fire on impact.' He gave a hopeless shrug. 'I was at work when the hospital called—in the middle of a meeting. Normally I would not be disturbed, but my PA called me out, said this was a call I needed to take. I knew it would be bad. I had no idea how bad, though—a doctor told me that Rico, Guido's father, was already dead, and that my sister was asking for me. I came straight away. Guido had been at a crèche and they'd brought him to the hospital.'

'I'm sorry.'

'She knew she was dying—she had terrible burns—but she was able to talk. She waited for me to get there so she could tell me what she wanted, so she could tell me herself the things Guido likes…'

'That was the list you were reading?'

He nodded, but it was a hopeless one. 'I love my sister, I love my nephew, but I have no idea how they really lived. I saw them often, but I have no clue with day-to-day things, I've never even thought of having children…'

'Is there anyone else?' Ainslie blinked, glimpsing how impossible it must be for him—for his whole life to be turned around, to be so suddenly plunged into grief and told you were to be a father.

'There was just my sister—our parents are dead.'

'But her husband's family…' It was never going to be

the easiest conversation to have—sitting with a stranger who was engulfed by grief and exhaustion—it was always going to be difficult. But, watching his face harden, hearing his sharp intake of breath, even if she didn't know him at all, Ainslie knew she had said the wrong thing.

'Never!' The venom behind the single world had Ainslie reeling.

'Soon they will be here. Already they are making noises about taking care of Guido, and noises are all I will let them be. They are not interested in him.'

'But they say they want him?' Ainslie frowned, her mouth opening to speak again, and then she got it. As he flicked his hand at their impressive surroundings, she answered in her head the question she hadn't even asked yet.

Elijah answered it with words. 'They want this. And the insurance pay-out—and the property Maria and Rico had in Italy…' He glanced over to her. 'And in case you are wondering—I do not need it…' He drained his mug. 'Neither do I need a toddler. Especially one who spits!' In the pit of his grief he managed to smile at the memory, and then it faded; his voice was pensive when next it came. 'I hope Rico knew that I did actually like him.'

She didn't understand, but it wasn't right to ask—wasn't right to demand more information from a man who had lost so much, a man who had just been plunged into hell.

'You should try and sleep,' Ainslie offered instead.

'Why?' He stared back at her. 'Somehow I do not believe that things will be better in the morning.'

'They might…' Ainslie attempted, but it was pretty futile.

'Thank you…' He said it again, only it was more deter-mined now. He was back in control and, ready to face the challenge of what lay ahead, he stood up. 'Thank you for explaining about the medicine and for helping me to get him to sleep. I will be fine now. Can I get you a taxi…?'

'Actually…' Ainslie ran a worried hand through her hair. She had been so consumed with his problems that for a little while she'd actually forgotten her own.

'Do you know a number?'

'Sorry?'

He was picking up the phone. 'For the taxi—do you know a number?'

'I can walk.' Ainslie's voice was a croak, but she cleared her throat. Surely a youth hostel would still be open? Surely?

'You're not walking!' Elijah shook his head. 'I will take…' He must have remembered at that point the sleeping toddler upstairs, because his voice trailed off. 'I insist you take a taxi.' Which was easier said than done. First he had to find a telephone directory, and then, as Ainslie stood there, he punched in the numbers and looked over. 'To where?'

'The youth hostel.'

'Youth hostel?' He frowned at her skirt and boots, at her twenty-eight-year-old face and glanced at his watch. In those two small gestures he compounded every one of her fears—she wasn't a backpacker, and nine p.m. on a dark December night was too late to start acting like one. 'How long have you been staying there?'

'I haven't.' Ainslie gave a tight shrug. 'I was on my way there when we met. I'm actually from Australia…'

'I have just come from Italy—first class,' he added, 'and I looked more dishevelled than you when I got off the plane.'

Somehow she doubted it, but she understood the point he was making.

'Well, I've been here for three months. I have a job—*had* a job…'

'Working with children?'

'That's right.'

'But not now?' She shook her head, loath to elaborate, but thankfully he sensed her unwillingness and didn't push.

'Stay.' It was an offer, not a plea. The phone rested on his shoulder as he affirmed his offer. 'Stay for tonight—as you say, tomorrow things may seem better.'

Ainslie opened her mouth to tell him why she couldn't possibly—only nothing came out.

Even if a hostel was open, even if she could get in one, the thought of registering, the thought of starting again, of greeting strangers, lying in a bed in a room for six, held utterly no appeal.

'Stay!' Elijah said more firmly. 'Guido is sick—it makes sense.'

It made no sense.

Not a single scrap of sense.

But somehow it did.

CHAPTER THREE

THOUGH he never voiced it, Ainslie knew and could understand that he didn't want to be alone. Jangling with nerves after the day's events, while simultaneously drooping with exhaustion, she sat on the sofa, tucked her legs under her and stifled a yawn as Elijah located two glasses and poured them both a vast brandy. Even though she didn't particularly like the taste, she accepted it, screwing up her nose as she took a sip, the warmth spreading down her throat to her stomach. She knew there and then why it was called medicinal—for the first time since she'd caught Gemma in between the sheets the adrenaline that had propelled her dimmed slightly, and she actually relaxed a touch—till he asked her a question.

'You said you worked with children?'

'I'm a kindergarten teacher—well, I am in Australia. Here I've been working as a live-in nanny.'

'Why?' Elijah frowned.

'Why not?' Ainslie retorted—though he was hardly the first to ask. Why would she give up a perfectly nice job, walk out on her perfectly nice boyfriend, and travel to the other side of the world to be paid peanuts to live in someone else's home and look after their kids?

'What were you running away from?'

'I wasn't running…' Ainslie bristled, and then, because he had been honest, somehow she could be more honest with this stranger than she had been with her own family. 'I suppose I *was* running away—only I didn't know from what at the time. I had a nice job, a lovely boyfriend, nice everything, really…'

'But?'

'Something wasn't right.' Ainslie gave a tight shrug. 'It was nothing I could put my finger on, but it turns out my instincts were right.'

'In what way?'

Shrewd eyes narrowed on her as she stiffened, and Elijah didn't push as, with a shake of her head, Ainslie stared into her glass and declined to elaborate. 'Everyone said I was crazy, that I'd regret it, but coming to London was the best thing I've ever done—I've loved every minute.'

'So why were you standing on the platform crying?' Elijah asked, and her eyes flew back to his. She was surprised he'd even noticed. 'And why are you checking into a youth hostel so late in the evening?'

'Things didn't work out with my boss…' Ainslie attempted casual, but those astute eyes were still watching her carefully. 'I'll find something else.'

'You already have,' Elijah answered easily. 'I don't know how long it will be for, but I'm certainly going to be here till after Christmas…'

'You don't know me…' Ainslie frowned.

'I won't know the girl the agency sends tomorrow either!' he pointed out. 'The offer's there if you want it.'

'Won't his father's family want to help out?' She could see him bristle—see him tense, just as he had before when they were mentioned.

He was about to tell her it was none of her business—about to snap some smart response—but those green eyes that beckoned him weren't judging, and there was no trace of nosiness in her voice. Elijah realised he didn't want to push her away, didn't want to be alone. For the first time in his life he actually needed to talk.

'Our families have never got on. When Maria started going out with Rico I didn't talk to my sister for two years.'

'Were you close before that?'

'We were all the other had. I was five when my mother died; Maria was only one. Our father turned to drink, and he died when I was twelve.'

He'd never told anyone this—could scarcely believe the words were coming out of his own mouth. Her jade-green eyes hardly ever left his. Every now and then she looked away, swirling her brandy in her glass as he spoke, but her gaze always returned to him. Her damp blonde hair was drying now, coiling into curls on her shoulders, and for the first time he walked through the murky depths of his past in the hope that it would guide him to the right future, that the decisions that must surely be made now would be the right ones for Guido.

'We brought ourselves up,' Elijah explained. 'Did things that today I am not proud of. But at the time…' He gave a regretful shrug. 'There was a family in our village—the Castellas. They were as rough as us, and after the same thing—money to survive. You could say we were rivals, I guess. One day Rico's older brother Marco came on to Maria.' His eyes flinched at the memory. 'She was still a child—thirteen—and she was an innocent child too. I had always been the one who did the cheating and stealing while Maria went to school; she was a good girl. Maria always hated Marco for what he did to her; she would not want him near Guido.'

'So this isn't about revenge?'

'I had my revenge the day it happened,' Elijah said darkly. 'I beat him to a pulp.'

'So the hatred just grew?' Ainslie asked, but Elijah didn't answer directly.

'When I was seventeen I was outside a café, watching some rich tourists. It was a couple, and I was waiting till it was darker, till they'd had a few more drinks and wouldn't be paying close attention to their wallets. They spoke to the waiter. Their Italian was quite good—they were looking to retire, wanted a property with a view…' He smiled at the memory. 'There was no estate agent in our small village in Sicily then—it wasn't a tourist spot. I knew, I just knew, that I didn't want to be stealing and cheating to get by any more. Finally I knew what I could do to get out of it.'

She didn't comment further, didn't frown at the fact that he'd stolen, didn't wince at his past, and that gave him the strength to continue.

'I sold them my late grandfather's home—to me and to my friends it was a shack, just a deserted place we hung out in. It had been passed to us, Maria and me, but till then it had been worth nothing. But we cleaned it painted and polished it, and Maria picked flowers for the inside. I could see what they wanted, and knew that this villa was it.'

'*You* sold it to them?'

'They dealt with the lawyers, they had the papers drawn up.' Elijah nodded. 'Then, after that, I sold our own home. With every bit of money I made I bought more properties, then I moved out of our village and on to bigger things—and the Castellas were still there, thieving on the beach. With every success that came our way they hated us more—just as we hated them.'

'You're a real estate agent?' Ainslie checked, wondering why that made him smile.

'I'm a property developer. I buy homes like this one—beautiful homes the world over—and I retain the exterior, gut the interior, and turn them into flats.'

'Ouch!' Ainslie winced, staring around at this vast lounge, the size of a ballroom, at the ornate cornices and the marble mantelpiece over the dreamy fireplace, loath to think of it being destroyed.

'Of course we try to retain as many original features as possible!' He gave an ironic smile.

'Philistine.'

'Perhaps!' Elijah conceded. 'Maria, too, fell in love with this place.'

'And she fell in love with Rico too?'

After the longest time he nodded, that single gesture telling her he would reveal more.

'Not till years later. I was furious—so too was his family. None of us went to the wedding...' He closed his eyes in regret. 'She still worked for me, supported her husband. I kept pointing out that he wasn't working, but slowly I started to see that they were for real. They had to be real. Because in spite of what had happened—with all that his brother had done—still she loved Rico. So we started speaking again, and then I realised how hard things were for them. Rico's family blamed Maria for what had happened to them, for the slur to Marco's name. They said that she had asked for it, that it had been her coming on to him…'

'She was thirteen!'

'Easier for them to blame her than change him. Rico is a mechanic, and his family ran the car repair place in the village, so he couldn't work. I knew they couldn't stay in the village—there was too much bad blood, too many slurs for them to ever make a real go of it. I suggested they move in here for a while—Maria spoke some English. I had purchased the place furnished, and I said she could oversee the plans, help with the architects and inspections till it was ready to get off the ground. It never did.' He smiled as he said it. 'The renovations started—only not the ones I had intended—Rico found work straight away, and they settled right in. I would often come to visit…'

'You were living in London?'

'No, I am mainly in Italy. But I am here once or twice a month, and every time I came here I noticed it had become more and more their home—a few new cushions for the couches, a rug here and there. And then when she got pregnant Maria started talking about a mural in the nursery. I gave in when Guido was born. I knew that they loved each other completely, and as a belated wedding gift I decided to sign the place over to them.'

'Some wedding gift!'

'Oh, it was to be their Christmas present too!'

Ainslie smiled at the faint joke. She knew nothing about property prices, save that London was fiercely expensive. She'd thought Gemma and Angus lived in luxury, but this house, right in the heart of London, was just stunning. Under any other circumstances she'd have paid to enter and be gazing at this lounge from behind a red rope! Ainslie gulped, staring over at the man sitting beside her on the couch. And under any other circumstances she'd be gazing at him on the silver screen, or in a glossy magazine.

Effortlessly stunning, he was quite simply the most beautiful man she had ever witnessed in the flesh. The features that had first dazzled her on the tube merited closer inspection now.

His jet hair was thick and glossy, and there was a slightly depraved look to his piercing blue eyes—but that could, Ainslie conceded, be more born of exhaustion than excess. His very straight Roman nose was a proud feature. All his features were wonderful in their own right, yet combined they were stunning. But what moved Ainslie most, what exalted him from good-looking to stunning, were the full lips of his mouth—the curve of them when he smiled. It was a mouth that softened his features, a mouth that flexed around his expressive language, a mouth that drew you closer, that held your attention when he spoke.

'It felt right that she have this house. Right that I could take care of her still. She's my sister—*was* my sister…' His voice husked, his mouth struggling with the correction.

'She still is…' Ainslie said softly. 'Always will be.'

'This place was their home. It is right that it's Guido's home now.'

'What will you do?'

'I don't know.' He stared into the bottom of his near-empty glass as if he were trying to gaze into a crystal ball. 'Marco and his wife, Dina, have never seen him, have played no part in his life, and yet now Rico and Maria are dead they say they want to be involved.'

'Were *you* involved?'

'I've never babysat, never changed his nappy...' Elijah answered. 'But I spoke with my sister on the phone most days. As I said, I'm in London once or maybe twice a month, and I normally stopped by. I was—am—a part of his life. It just never entered my head it would be to this extent.'

'It might be the same for Marco and Dina,' Ainslie offered. 'Maybe they've had a shock? Maybe they've realised...?' Her voice trailed off as he shook his head.

'I don't trust them.' He drained the last dregs before continuing, 'I don't want that man near my nephew—he is the last person Maria would want for him. I know people can change, and I know that it was a long time ago. But some things—well, they are too hard to excuse or forgive.'

'There's no one else?'

'No one apart from one reprobate uncle who likes to burn the candle at both ends and has an appalling track record with women.'

'Oh!' Ainslie blinked, rather liking the sound of him. 'Where's he, then?'

'You're looking at him.' He even managed to laugh, but it faded quickly. 'The trouble is, as wrong as I think Marco and Dina would be for him, I don't trust that I am right for Guido either. I don't have a lifestyle that really fits in with raising a child. I can provide for him, I can give him the best of everything...'

But he deserved so much more than that, and they both knew it.

'It might be time to grow up, I guess!' Elijah said, putting down his glass and standing. 'Either that or try and find a way to put aside lifelong rivalries and remember it isn't a patch on the beach we're fighting over any more.'

'You'll work it out.'

'Just not tonight…'

They shuffled through the house and up the stairs.

'This is a guest room,' Elijah announced. 'And there's another one here.' Elijah pushed open another door. 'You can choose.'

'I don't care…'

Ainslie shrugged, so he chose for her, depositing her backpack in a pretty yellow and white room that was to be her home for tonight.

'I'll just check on Guido.'

They both did.

Stood in his parents' bedroom and peered into his cot. His flushed face was paler now, his thumb was in his mouth and his bottom was in the air, and tears welled in Ainslie's eyes as she stared down at him. Safe and warm but suddenly alone, without the two people who would have loved him the most. The vast bed in the room looked horribly empty as they crept out.

'Will we wake up?' As he turned to go he thought better of it. 'Who will wake up to Guido?'

And it was a very sensible question. Babies who woke in the night wouldn't usually be factored in to Elijah Vanaldi's agenda. Little whimpers of distress wouldn't necessarily jerk a man like him from slumber.

'I'll wake.' Ainslie smiled softly at his exhausted face. 'You should try and get some rest.'

She'd wake if only first she could sleep.

Her head was racing at a million miles an hour as she lay in the strange bed, listening as Elijah showered. Familiar sounds in an unfamiliar place, and for the first time since she'd put the key in the front door this afternoon she was able to draw breath.

To actually think about what she should do with her own situation.

If she pleaded her case Gemma had made it clear that without warning or hesitation she would call the police, and Ainslie knew that no one would employ a childcare worker who was being investigated. Even if she could prove her innocence, the slur alone would be enough to ruin her time in England. Elijah had offered her a position, but for how long? A day? A week? How long would it be till he went back to Italy?

Ainslie blinked into the darkness. He was trusting her to help him—what would he say if he knew that she had been accused of theft?

As the shrill screams of Guido pierced the night Elijah sat up, gulping in air as he awoke from a nightmare...

His sister had been dead—no, she'd been dying—her body horribly disfigured, her voice a strained, hoarse whisper as she'd tried to speak through her swollen and damaged windpipe, imploring him to listen, warning him of the Castellas descending, claiming her baby, taking what they considered theirs. He'd gone to hold her hand, to tell her it was all okay, that he would take care of things. Only her hand… He could feel bile rising in his throat as he replayed the image.

It was just a dream, Elijah assured himself, sheathed in sweat, and trying to pull himself out of it. A nightmare. The horrible panic, the utter dread with which he'd awoken should be abating now, should be dimming as reality filtered in. Instead, Elijah could feel his heart quicken as he took in his surrounds. Another shot of adrenaline propelled him out of bed in panic. He grabbed a towel and wrapped it around his hips, dashing to his nephew as he realised he hadn't awoken *from* a nightmare—he was living one.

'He's okay!'

It was like falling off a cliff into soft outstretched arms. Ainslie was leaning over Guido's cot, pressing her finger to her lips to tell him to be quiet, dressed in vast, shapeless pyjamas that were covered in some pattern he couldn't make out. Guido's little night light caught the gold in her blonde hair as briefly she looked up from the child she soothed, her voice soft and calming—not just to Guido, but to himself.

Only Ainslie herself wasn't soothed. Clemmie and Jack had both regularly woken in the night and, used to sleeping light, she'd woken when Guido had first whimpered. She had been stumbling down the hall by the time his screaming had started, and had been able to quickly soothe him— deliberately not turning on the light, so her strange presence wouldn't alarm him. Instead she'd replaced his blanket, as Elijah had mentioned, and patting his back had gently hushed him. And then Elijah had come to the door, breathless, as if he'd been running.

'He's nearly back to sleep,' she whispered as he came over quietly. Ainslie lowered her head back into the crib.

Suddenly she was glad for the dim lighting in the room, because her face was one burning blush at the sight of Elijah wearing nothing more than a towel, and she was absolutely aware of his presence as he stood beside her till she was happy that Guido was asleep.

Of course he'd be wearing nothing, Ainslie scolded herself as they crept out of the bedroom. He hadn't exactly had time to pack, and she couldn't somehow see a man like Elijah rummaging through his dead brother-in-law's clothes to find something to wear.

But that wasn't the problem and she knew it—hell, she'd caught Angus, her old employer, on the landing in nothing more than a pair of boxers loads of times, and it had done nothing for her, nothing at all, had barely merited a thought. But walking along the landing behind Elijah, seeing the taut definition of his muscled back, the silky olive skin, inhaling the soapy masculine scent of him, well, it merited more than just a thought.

'Goodnight.' He turned to face her, his hair all rumpled from falling asleep with it wet, still unshaven, his incredibly beautiful eyes dark wells of anguish as he hesitated to go. 'Do you think he knows? Do you think he knows that they are gone?'

'On some level, perhaps.' She was helpless to comfort him—had been wondering the same thing herself as she'd soothed the little boy back to sleep. 'He'll know things are different, he'll be unsettled and he'll want his parents. But so long as his little world is safe he'll be okay.'

'Will he remember them?' He delivered a slightly mocking laugh to himself. 'Of course he won't.'

'I don't agree,' Ainslie said gently, because it was up to

Elijah now to turn the fragile images Guido held and somehow merge them into his life. 'I mean, there will be pictures, DVDs with them on it that he can watch over and over. I don't know much about child grief, but I think…'

'I can hardly remember,' Elijah said, explaining the mocking laugh. 'I can hardly remember my mother at all—and she died when I was five. Guido is not even two. He's only fifteen months old.'

'Did your father talk to you about her?' Ainslie pushed, but she already knew the answer. 'You can make it different for Guido.'

'Can I?'

Her hand instinctively reached out for his arm, touching him as she would anyone in so much pain. Only the contact, the feeling of his skin beneath her fingers, the hairs on his arm, the satin of his skin against her palm, the touch that had been offered as comfort, shifted to something else entirely as her eyes jerked to his.

At any point she could have reclaimed her hand. At any point she could have said goodnight and gone back to her room. Only she didn't—couldn't. The air thrummed with the thick scent of arousal—grief and shock a strange propellant, one that forced a million emotions into the air in one very direct hit, accelerating feelings and blurring boundaries. The day that had left them both reeling, forced them to go through the motions, to run on sheer adrenaline, was at an end now, and now they paused—paused long enough to draw breath before the impossible race started again. A race neither wanted to resume.

Just easier, far easier, to ignore the pain for a moment, to stand and instead of facing the future face each other.

Elijah stared into her eyes as he tried to picture the last few hours without her in it. Always he had a solution—another plan to initiate if things didn't go his way. There was nothing that truly daunted him. But walking out of that hospital, holding his nephew in his arms, he had felt the weight of responsibility overwhelm him. Gripped with fear, not for himself but for Guido, he had had no glimmer of a plan, no thought process to follow, had just clung on to his nephew as he'd clung to *him*. And then she had come along—an angel descending when he'd needed it most. And he needed her now.

'Why did you stop?' His voice was low, his question important.

'Why wouldn't I stop?' Ainslie blinked. 'You needed help.'

'But no one else did.'

Hundreds had passed him that day—had jammed against him on the underground, hadn't made room as he'd lifted the stroller, had squashed into Guido as if they didn't even notice he was there. At the platform before he'd met her many had seen him struggle, and out of all of them she was the only one who had tried to help. He didn't want to picture how this night would have been without her kind concern. Didn't want to envisage stepping into this house alone with Guido. Didn't want to think about any of it for even a second longer…

His breath was getting faster now, the nightmare coming back, and he struggled to surface from it, to drag in air and escape. He needed her now just as much, if not more, than then. He drew comfort in the only way he knew how. He lowered his mouth and claimed hers, the bliss of contact fulfilling a craving, a need for escape—such a balmy escape—the medicine so sweet, the feel of her in his arms like a haven.

For a second she resisted, fought the urge to kiss him back. The speed of it all, the inappropriateness, flitted into her mind, then flitted out—because maybe she craved oblivion too. As his tongue parted her lips and his skilled mouth searched hers Ainslie thought that maybe it was because she'd never been so thoroughly kissed before. The wretched, wretched day was fading—the sting of Gemma's accusations, the panic and fear that had gripped her when she'd found herself alone in a strange city—all was abating as with his mouth he soothed and excited.

In this crazy day he had helped her too—was helping her now.

This heady, blinding kiss was frenzied almost—like an anaesthetic, dousing pain, dimming thought. His hands knotted in her hair as he drank from her mouth, his mouth so hot on hers there was a delicious hurt. Deep lusty kisses both claimed and bestowed, and each breath she took was his, each breath she gave he gulped in. It was a dangerous kiss that could only lead to more. Yet somehow he made her feel safe, his strong arms holding her, his hands clutching her to him, his lips grazing her neck, the scratch of his chin on her sensitive skin making her weak. She'd never been kissed like this before—never been wanted or wanted so badly herself. The heady rush fizzed in her veins, racing around her body—stroking her pelvic floor like an inner caress. And it had to stop, because if it didn't then they wouldn't.

Pulling back her head, though his arms still circled her body, she called a reluctant halt. Both were staring, both breathing as if they had run a mile. The delicious shock doused her, her own body's response astonished her—

every encounter in her life laid end to end didn't come close to matching this.

'Don't…' He husked his response to her unvoiced statement—disparity evident as her body thrummed in his arms.

'I have to.' She could hardly speak, her whole body so drenched with arousal, so utterly opposed to her mind, that it took every ounce of effort she possessed to walk from his room, to lie on her bed…to walk away from his.

It was just a kiss. She told herself. *A kiss because…*

Only she couldn't answer that one. Ainslie's fingers moved to her mouth, feeling it swollen where his lips had been. She could still feel the tender flesh of her neck where his chin had made her raw.

And it wasn't just a kiss—kisses had never left her weak like that; kisses had never left her lost. Which she had been, completely lost in the moment with him.

She tried to put it out of her mind, to focus on her problems instead of letting her imagination wander, to tell herself to let it go.

But her body said otherwise. And the slightly open bedroom doors channelled their want as they both lay alone in the oppressive silence. Ainslie, her body twitching with desire and thick, greedy need, lay there rigid, almost in desperation for the escape they had briefly found, willing herself to relax, to sleep. Trying to ignore the man who lay just metres away, who was, after one kiss, the only man who had utterly moved her.

CHAPTER FOUR

'WHEN did all that come?' Exhausted, dishevelled, and still coming to terms with yesterday, Ainslie had tripped over a pile of luxury luggage in the hall.

'While you were sleeping,' Elijah said, not looking up. Dressed only in a pair of grey hipsters, unshaven and tousled, he still managed to look absurdly sexy as he shared a bowl of cereal with Guido—one spoon for his nephew, then a larger one for Elijah. 'I arranged some belongings to be couriered over yesterday.' He glanced up at her raised eyebrows—raised because, with all that had taken place, how could he even think about clothes? 'I couldn't face putting on my suit again today.'

'Oh!' Ainslie said, feeling horribly small all of a sudden, as she tried to work out the kitchen. She knew how adrift *she* felt without all of her belongings—but at least she had clean knickers.

Elijah turned to face her. 'I've also arranged a driver—Tony. He's going to be staying in a room on the third floor, so he's available whenever you need him—that is if you stay.'

'A live-in driver!'

'It's impossible to park in London.' Elijah shrugged, lying easily. She didn't need to know he'd actually arranged a bodyguard for Guido—there was no way he was risking the Castellas coming to take him. 'And I don't like walking. Actually,' he conceded slightly, 'he's just broken up with his wife and he needs a live-in job. It was either him or rely on taxis.'

'You've been busy.'

'I always am.' Elijah waited till she came over before continuing. 'Look, I really don't want to push, but I need to know if you are willing to work for me.'

His eyes met hers when finally she joined him at the breakfast table. There had been no mention of what had taken place last night. He'd shown not a trace of awkward-ness when he'd greeted her. In fact he was so cool, so com-pletely together, Ainslie even wondered if she'd imagined the whole thing—like some strange erotic dream that made her blush to think about it. She was actually starting to wonder if anything *had* happened, because Elijah didn't look at all fazed or embarrassed.

Or maybe he was just used to it, Ainslie mused as she sugared her coffee. Perhaps he was so used to snogging the hired help whenever it took his fancy it didn't merit a second thought.

It had merited more than a second thought for Ainslie. Problems like finding work and somewhere to live in a strange country just a few days before Christmas, like coming up with some quick money to pay off her debt, had all become mere irrelevancies as she'd lain in bed and relived his kiss over and over.

And now he was asking for an answer as to whether she

would work for him—an answer that, on several levels, she was hesitant to give.

'Can I have some time to think about it?'

'Unfortunately, no—I have already received a rather irate call from Guido's case worker. It would seem that I should not have taken him without the Social Services department's approval.'

'Well, that would have gone down well!' Ainslie couldn't keep the note of sarcasm out of her voice.

'It didn't.'

'So how did you respond?'

'I said that perhaps they should question their procedures rather than me!' He gave a tight smile. 'That didn't go down too well either! And Marco and his wife, Dina, have arrived, and have made it clear that they will be applying for custody. Guido's case worker is coming to meet with me here this morning—it would be helpful to say that I already have arranged childcare, and if you can't work for me I can at least call an agency and be able to say that I have lined up some interviews.'

'I understand that…' Ainslie stirred honey into some porridge and attempted to feed a less than impressed Guido, who was far happier sharing his uncle's bowl. 'I just don't think it's going to be possible for me to work for you.'

'Because you have another job to go to?' She could hear the sarcasm in his voice.

'No.'

'Because you would rather spend Christmas in a youth hostel?'

His arrogance didn't faze her.

'Maybe because I'd prefer to have a few days off over

Christmas and New Year rather than being treated like dirt while I mind some rich family's child!' She gave him a sweet smile over Guido's porridge, but it didn't meet her eyes. They both knew that wasn't the reason.

'I would not treat you badly. And there would be no repeat…' He didn't elaborate. He didn't have to. The colour roared up her cheeks as for a dangerous second they both revisited last night, as her erotic dream was confirmed as reality. 'The top floor is self contained—you could have that. We could draw up a contract…'

'That's not the only issue…' Ainslie swallowed hard, her face burning as she wondered if a lie was a lie if it was by omission. It would be so, so easy to accept his offer. The thought of spending Christmas at a youth hostel, of searching for work at the most impossible time of the year, was daunting to say the least. She knew Elijah was desperate, that he probably wouldn't get around to checking her references for a while, but still integrity won, and Ainslie knew she had somehow to tell him her truth without revealing Gemma's indiscretion. 'You might not want me looking after Guido.' Two vertical lines deepened on the bridge of his nose, but that was the only reaction she took in before she quickly looked away. 'It wasn't a mutual parting of ways—I was actually sacked yesterday.'

'For?'

It was a reasonable question—a *very* reasonable question—and one Ainslie didn't know how to answer. To tell him the truth, the whole truth, felt disloyal to Angus and especially to the children—privileged information gathered when you worked in someone's home, whether good or bad, wasn't hers to divulge. Yet to be labelled a thief, to have her own reputation tarnished, posed for Ainslie an impossible conundrum.

The shrill of her mobile broke the strained silence, and Ainslie cringed when she saw it was Angus.

'Ainslie?' His voice was worried. 'Where are you?'

'I'm fine.'

'What happened?'

'Just leave it, Angus.' Her face was one burning blush. She was wishing, wishing Elijah would show some manners, would get up and leave the table so she could take this exquisitely difficult phone call in private.

'I can't just leave it. Gemma says things have been going missing for weeks…is that true?'

And here was the horrible junction one invariably came to when lying—to claw back from the pit and admit the painful truth, or to cross the point of no return and fully embark on a lie.

'Look, Angus…just give me a moment…'

Despite giving him a rather pointed look, it was clear Elijah wasn't going anywhere, so it was Ainslie who left the table and headed into the kitchen. Closing the door, she let out a long breath, wondering what on earth she could say to make things if not better for herself then no worse for him. For Angus to believe her she had to lie convincingly—it was that or let him know his wife was cheating.

'You know I needed money.' She screwed her eyes closed as she said it. 'Nick hasn't kept up with the loan payments. I didn't think Gemma would miss a few things.'

'Ainslie—this just doesn't sound like you—you're one of the most honest people I've met, and the kids just adored you. I thought you were happy working with them…'

He didn't believe her—wouldn't take the out she was offering. So, taking a deep breath, Ainslie attempted to be more convincing, tried adding a bit of spite to her voice as tears streamed down her face.

'Well, I wasn't happy, actually! And I got sick of seeing Gemma parading her nice things. I decided I wanted some nice things too. I'm surprised she even noticed the necklace was gone—it's not as if she's spoilt for choice.'

There was a horribly long silence, but that was preferable to hearing him speak—the disappointment evident in his voice as he bought her lie.

'Where are you now?'

'Don't worry about me.'

'Unfortunately I do.' Angus let out a tired sigh. 'We owe you some wages—and there's your Christmas bonus…'

'I'm not going to be working for Christmas.'

'You've been great with the kids these last three months—and you've done a lot of babysitting at short notice. I'd rather do this right.' Angus's voice was resigned. 'Look, can we meet? I'll bring the rest of your things and—I'm sorry, Ainslie—Gemma wants the phone back. And—well—the kids were pretty upset. They've made you a card…'

'I'm sorry, Angus…' Her voice was thick with tears.

'Meet me in half an hour.'

'That was my boss.' Red-eyed, Ainslie returned to the table, where Elijah was sipping on disgustingly strong coffee. 'My old boss,' she corrected. 'I have to go and meet him.'

'To obtain a reference?' Tongue firmly in cheek, Elijah looked at her—and she knew, just knew, what he was thinking. Her employment had ended because she'd been found having an affair with her boss. If only he knew the truth!

'I doubt it somehow.'

'Did your termination have anything to do with your work with the children?'

'No.'

He watched a salty fat tear spill down her cheek.

'His wife—well, she wanted me gone. She said that I...'

Her voice trailed off. She knew, just knew, what Elijah must be thinking and struggled to rectify it. 'It's not what it seems.'

'It never is!' Elijah said dryly, and she gave a helpless shake of her head. 'So what happened?'

'I'd rather not say.'

'You're behind with a loan?'

'You were listening!' Ainslie gasped, appalled not just that he had listened, but at how blatantly he'd admitted it.

Elijah just shrugged. 'I have no qualms listening through the door—not where my nephew's safety is concerned.'

'You had no right!'

'I don't see it that way—some of the best decisions I have made have been based on information others would rather I hadn't heard. So, I ask again—you are behind with a loan?'

Ainslie gave a miserable nod. 'I was relying on my Christmas bonus to make some payments.'

'And Nick is your ex? You have debts with him?'

'Debts I didn't know about...' Ainslie was struggling and failing not to cry. 'I found out a couple of weeks ago that he'd taken a loan out while were together—in both our names. I didn't know anything about it till I got some for-warded mail. He hasn't paid the last two payments, and I've rung him a few times and it doesn't sound as if he's got any intention of meeting them.'

'So now you've found out why you left him…' His insight halted her tears. 'Something really *wasn't* right. Have you contacted a lawyer?'

'A lawyer would probably end up costing more than the loan…' Ainslie gave a worried shake of her head. 'It's easier to just keep paying it for now. I've spoken to the bank, but they haven't been very helpful…'

'So you have a motive, and you've admitted to something you didn't do. The question remains, why would you admit to something you didn't do?'

Her eyes shot to his, her face colouring under his scrutiny. 'What do you mean? If you were listening properly you'd have heard me say that I did steal.'

'Thieves never admit, though.' Still he stared. 'I know because I was one—and I know that you are not.'

That he believed her, that somehow, despite all evidence to the contrary, he believed her, brought a fresh batch of tears to her eyes.

'So why did you just lie?'

'It's complicated…' His interrogation flailed her—his insight, his questions, confused her. She was tempted, so tempted to tell this stranger her truth, yet even knowing she couldn't, but that he believed her, brought strange comfort.

'Angus—he's a doctor. He's quite famous, actually; he's on television, in the news. When I took the job I signed a contract… I promised them that…' Ainslie shook her head. It was hopeless. 'Look, I'm sorry that I can't answer your questions, and understand that you may want to reconsider your offer. I have to go and meet Angus now—if I could leave my things for a couple of hours…?' God, why didn't he just say something—anything? Ainslie thought. His scrutiny was unnerving her.

But even when he answered he left her hanging.

'Guido's social worker will be arriving soon—I will let you know my decision on your return.'

He'd already made it. Whatever had gone on, or was still going on between herself and her old boss, at least she was discreet. For a man in Elijah's position, a female with discretion was a rare commodity—and one, amongst other things, he was going to need to win Guido's case worker over.

He'd met Ms Anderson at the hospital yesterday, and had disliked her instantly. Normally Elijah could charm any woman. He had flirted from the cradle, and quickly worked out that with the right flash of those blue eyes he instantly got his way—not with Ms Anderson.

'Your lifestyle really isn't suited to such a young child.' Ms Anderson got straight to the point once he'd shown her in. 'While I appreciate you can afford the best in childcare, what we are seeking for Guido is a more nurturing family environment for him to thrive. His uncle Marco and his wife, Dina, already have two children, and understand more what they are offering to take on…'

'My sister was explicit in her wish—and that was that *I* had custody of Guido.'

'Your sister was dying when she made that wish. She was no doubt in pain and emotional too…' Ms Anderson said, slightly more softly. 'And while of course her wishes must be taken into consideration, there are Guido's father's wishes to consider too.'

'His would have been the same.'

'Without a will, we'll never know.'

'*I* know!' Elijah flared, but fought it. He knew he had to keep his emotions in check if he was going to put across his point. 'Rico didn't talk to his family—that is why they were here in London. They wanted to be away from them.'

'That's not what the Castellas told me.' As he opened his mouth to argue, Ms Anderson overrode him. 'I am not getting into a pointless debate of "he said, she said". In the absence of a will, all we can look after is the best interests of the child—that is our primary concern.'

'It is *my* primary concern too!'

'It wasn't yesterday!' Ms Anderson was resolute. 'You walked out of the hospital yesterday evening with Guido— you just took him…'

'There was no reason for him to be there. He wasn't involved in the car accident. He has an ear infection and croup! It hardly merits a hospital bed!'

'His immediate care was supposed to be discussed *prior* to his discharge.'

'He is my nephew.' Elijah glowered. 'You speak as if I kidnapped him, as if I am depriving him of medical care, when in fact, I told a hospital doctor my intentions, and he himself prescribed medicine.'

'You waited till the Social Services department was closed, though, and you spoke with a very junior doctor! I'm sure you can be quite intimidating when you want to be!' Ms Anderson held his glare. 'The department wants Guido's passport…'

'Well, they can't have it. I have no idea where it is.'

'Then it looks as if I might be here for a while. Do you want me to help you look?'

Of course it was in the second drawer she opened—there in the dresser, amongst wedding photos, birth and marriage certificates. Elijah's lips pursed. His clothes arriving, employing a supposed driver and a nanny, were all intended to make it look as if he were planning to stay—yet his intention *had* been to leave straight after the funeral. Back to his lawyers, his contacts, to the power he held in his home town—power that would cut through this senseless red tape in a matter of days. For a second Elijah rued the fact he hadn't headed straight for the airport this morning—but that wasn't going to get him anywhere. So instead of dwelling on a past that couldn't be altered, Elijah treated it as a business problem, handing over the passport without comment as he was forced to move swiftly to Plan B—or rather quickly come up with a Plan B.

'Surely he should be here…?' Elijah said, his hands gesturing to the impressive lounge. 'Here amongst familiar things? At least for now, till a decision is made…'

'It's a big house…'

Ms Anderson gave a nervous cough as Elijah's face hardened. Clearly the cosy family scenario she had just mentioned was not going to eventuate *here*.

'It is *my* house,' Elijah clipped.

'Your house?' Ms Anderson frowned, peering down at her notes. 'The Castellas said that it belonged to Maria and Rico—that they had just taken possession of the title.'

He was about to deliver a smart reply, but something halted him.

'They said that?' His mind was whirring at the fact that they would even *know*—but then his home town was small, and even if his lawyers were discreet, who knew about their secretaries, or the typist, or whoever was cleaning the desk? 'Don't you think it strange that within weeks of Maria and Rico—?'

'Mr Vanaldi…' Her voice bordered on the sympathetic. 'The police have said that the accident wasn't suspicious, and the Castellas were in Italy when it occurred.'

He was sounding irrational, Elijah knew that—but she didn't know the Castellas, or the levels they'd stoop to. Instead of arguing his point Elijah chose to play his cards close, to stay one step ahead just as he always did.

'I'm just tired…' he quickly retracted.

'Of course you are.'

'But our families really do not get on…' he said carefully. 'It would not be in Guido's best interests to have two feuding families taking care of him at this time.'

'Well, if you're not prepared to put aside your differences, then I'm going to have make the choice for you, and frankly, Mr Vanaldi, I have looked into your lifestyle…' She pulled a face as if she were sucking on a lemon. 'Yachts, international trips, homes all over the place, partying…' She gave another uncomfortable cough. 'And it would seem you have rather a lot of lady-friends. It really doesn't sound like the most stable of environments—but the Castellas have said that they are prepared to relocate to England, if necessary. They are willing to do whatever it takes to give Guido a proper, loving home.'

'To live off him—' Elijah sneered.

'Mr Vanaldi!' Ms Anderson broke in. 'Affluence doesn't come into it. It's not a question of being able to provide materially for Guido—it would seem that for this child that's the only thing I *don't* have to worry about.'

She was right—silently he stared over at her—affluence had *nothing* to do with this. His money, his lavish lifestyle, wasn't what was needed here. Elijah knew that, and he also knew it had nothing to do with pride or possession... His gaze drifted to the photos on the mantelpiece, to the smiling faces of his sister and her husband.

How he'd hated Rico when Maria had confessed she was dating him.

Hated that Maria had got involved with the Castellas.

Gypsies.

As he had once been.

Rough, tough survivors—ruthlessly knocking over anyone who stood in their way. But the incident between Maria and Marco had changed Elijah, made him realise that the life he was leading was not one he wished to pursue. His ability to survive, to thrive, to read people was put to better use now. Elijah was the one who had pulled himself up by the bootlaces from a dirt-poor upbringing and made something of himself.

And how the Castellas hated him for it.

Had hated Maria too.

Hated Rico for crossing to the other side.

And yet now suddenly they wanted Guido.

It would be so much easier for him to let Ms Anderson make the wrong decision... He could hear Guido stirring on the intercom system, and his jaw tightened at the mere prospect of the screams that would follow. Elijah Vanaldi was a man with not an ounce of paternal instinct. Yes, it would be infinitely easier to nod to the social worker, to say yes, Guido *would* be better off with a ready-made family—better off with his aunt and uncle and cousins—

only Elijah had never taken the easy option in life before, and he wasn't about to start now.

'I'm not going to go away, Ms Anderson. I am not going to give up on my nephew. You can do your research, you can rake as much dirt as you like on me—or I can save you the effort and tell you myself. I have a criminal record, mainly for petty theft and fighting—though there have been no further convictions since I turned seventeen. I'm sure that's not the case with Marco Castella. I have a lavish lifestyle that, yes, is probably not geared to raising a fifteen-month-old—but, given I didn't know I was going to be raising one, I trust that won't be held against me. And, yes, there have been many women. But, as I just pointed out, that was when I had no commitment to Guido. I will not step aside from this fight…'

'You do actually *want* what you're fighting for, don't you?' Ms Anderson angrily interrupted. 'Because if this is about winning a battle or proving a point, please remember that there is a child in the middle.'

He did—at every turn of his thoughts he did. He was honest enough with himself to know he wasn't perhaps the best choice as a parent for his nephew, but if it came down to him or the Castellas, like it or not, want it or not, he was the *only* choice.

Maria had never been able to stand Marco to be near her—there was no way on earth or in heaven she'd want him near her only child.

All he could do was his best for Guido.

Buy a little piece of time and use it to work out what was best.

Guido was crying now, waking from his nap and demanding a mother who wasn't there. Without excusing himself Elijah walked upstairs, into his sister's room, and stared over to where his nephew stood in the cot, coughing and crying and stinking to high heaven. Guido's outstretched arms pulled back when he saw it was his uncle, then the baby changed his mind and held them out again to be picked up.

What do you want me to do? Elijah didn't say it, just stared back into suspicious blue eyes, and he felt something twist inside, saw himself unwanted, ignored, told to clear off and play. And though he didn't want Guido to be used as a meal ticket for the Castellas, what he could offer was only the same in the extreme. With him, Guido's lifestyle would be peppered with nannies and first-class travel, and he knew that wasn't what this little boy needed.

'Che cosa lo desiderate fare?' This time he did say it out loud, only there could be no answer.

Picking up the little boy, feeling him rest his hot little head in his neck, the weight of responsibility in his arms was so heavy he almost buckled. Elijah wanted so badly to give his nephew the upbringing Maria would have chosen for him, wanted him to have always what Maria and himself had known only for a short while.

His eyes scanned Maria's dressing table, fixing on a shallow glass dish. Reaching out, he picked up a ring—his mother's ring—cheap Italian gold dotted with seed pearls and little bits of red glass. Despite what he'd told Ainslie last night, despite what he actually had believed, for the first time in the longest time he remembered—remembered his mum cooking, laughing, singing, remembered the short time when his life had been easy.

'*Da!*' Guido wriggled in his arms, pointing to the window, and Elijah gave a rare smile as he saw the first snow of winter whirring in the air and taking for ever to fall. He headed over to the window and looked at the billowing white flakes, melting into water before they even hit the ground.

And there was Ainslie—shivering in her flimsy jacket, pulling it down over her splendid bottom, dragging a vast case behind her. Her blonde hair was dark now, it was so wet, and something else twisted inside him—because despite the cold words he'd heard her say to Angus, she didn't look like the cool, calculated gold-digger he'd heard on the phone this morning.

And he didn't want her lost and alone in London at Christmas either.

'Lesson one,' he said lying Guido down on the change mat and trying not to look as he changed his first nappy. 'Sometimes you have to make things work your way, Guido.'

Ms Anderson listened as Elijah's thick Italian words came over the intercom, then got back to her notes. A good-looking playboy he might well be, but he was persuasive too. She'd had every intention of telling him that for Christmas at least Guido should stay with the Castellas—a charming family. She'd spoken to them at length before coming here, had helped them find the apartment they were renting, and was meeting them back at her office this afternoon. But hearing Elijah Vanaldi's surprisingly tender voice crackle over the speakers, then hearing him curse when he attempted to hold kicking legs still while he put on a nappy, Ms Anderson knew he wasn't playing to an audience. He would have forgotten about the intercom the second he left the room, and she knew that she really was listening to him interact with his nephew. Now, hearing the baby laugh, hearing Guido giggle and shriek as his uncle playfully scolded him for the *odore,* it was how it should be—a baby giggling and laughing, utterly oblivious to the tragedy unfolding around him. Something inside her shifted.

Her already heavy schedule was weightier now.

This wasn't going to be as cut and dried as she'd first hoped.

'Blasted snow!'

Since her trip to England had been but a glimmer in her eyes, Ainslie had dreamed of the proverbial white Christmas—had actually planned her trip so that she would arrive here in time for winter. Had it worked out with the Maitlins she'd have been heading off with them on her first ever skiing holiday in the New Year, but as snow swirled around her, soaked through her jacket, fell on her face, already raw and red from crying, all it did was sting… Angus had been lovely, which had made it worse somehow. He had given her more than a month's pay, plus her Christmas bonus, and had even, probably against his better judgement, given her a reference.

But what good was a reference a week before Christmas?

She'd checked out the local youth hostel and it looked as busy and exciting as her guidebook promised. She'd been told that a shared dorm *should* be available later in the day—only it was the last place she wanted to be right now. After the hell of the past two days she wanted some-where quiet, where she could lick her wounds and regroup…but where? On a limited budget, and with not much chance of getting immediate work, she wasn't exactly spoilt for choice.

Lugging her case up the steps, Ainslie decided to be brave, to ask Elijah if his offer still stood—just for a few days at least.

Rehearsing her speech, Ainslie stood on the doorstep, but before she'd even knocked the door was flung open.

Elijah pulled her into the warm as Guido ran down the hall in a nappy that was falling off and a T-shirt that was on inside out.

'You've been gone ages…'

'Really? Was I?'

'And you're frozen…' His hands were pulling at her jacket, taking off the damp garment as Ainslie spun in confusion at his effusive greeting. 'You're soaked.'

'Elijah, what on—?' She never got to finish, never got to say another word, because his mouth was on hers, his flesh pressing hers, his skin warm against her frozen cheeks. He was pinning her against the wall, kissing her cheeks, her eyes, as he took her icy hands. Then, just as she regrouped and opened her mouth to speak, his lips hushed her again. She could feel him pressing a ring on her finger. The whole intoxicating, dizzying contact took seconds, perhaps, but was utterly, utterly spinning her mind. This kiss was nothing, *nothing* like the one they had shared last night, and she pushed him back, her eyes frightened by his fervour—till they met his. She frowned at the silent plea she saw there…and then another presence was making itself known, a figure in the peripheries of her vision walking down the hall.

'Ms Anderson!' Elijah's hand gripped hers tightly. 'This is Ainslie…'

'Ainslie?' The middle-aged woman was picking up Guido. Maybe she was an aunt Elijah had discovered? Maybe Rico's relatives had arrived and they were talking? Or a neighbour, perhaps? All these thoughts whirred through Ainslie's head as she offered her hand to greet the woman.

'Is this the nanny?' Ms Anderson asked.

'The nanny?' Elijah let out a slightly incredulous laugh. 'Heavens, no—didn't I tell you? Ainslie is my fiancée.'

CHAPTER FIVE

'YOUR fiancée!' The wary, slightly sour expression on the prim, middle-aged face, faded in an instant. 'You're engaged? But why on earth didn't you say?'

'I didn't think to…' Elijah was still holding her hand, his eyes catching Ainslie's, almost daring her to refute him. 'I'm sorry—of course you would need to know these things. I just never thought. I've had so much—we've had so much on our minds.'

'And how does your fiancée feel…? I'm sorry.' She frowned over to Ainslie. 'I didn't introduce myself. I'm Rita Anderson, Guido's case worker—we were just trying to sort out Guido's short-term care, while we make a decision for the long term.'

'Ainslie Farrell.' Her eyes darted to Elijah, then back to Ms Anderson, her head whirring as Ms Anderson's eyes fell on the ring Ainslie now had on her finger.

'My—that's unusual!'

It certainly was, Ainslie thought as for the first time she eyed 'her' ring. Elijah's improvisation skills were rather lacking, because he might not have pulled it out of a

Christmas cracker, but it came close—certainly not the usual choice of ring for a billionaire's fiancée!

'It was my mother's.' Elijah explained, which actually made Ms Anderson's first smile even bigger.

'How lovely. So, how long have you two been engaged?'

'A few weeks.' How easily he lied.

'And how does your fiancée feel about all this?' Ms Anderson's gaze fell directly on Ainslie as she asked Elijah a question. 'Have you two spoken about taking on Guido?'

'There hasn't been much time for talking,' Ainslie answered in truthfulness. 'In fact…' she shot a look at Elijah '…I'm a bit stunned by it all.'

'Naturally she is overwhelmed.' Elijah took over the conversation. 'We both are. Ms Anderson, this has been a shock to us—we are trying to adjust, trying to work out what is best for Guido. For now surely that is for him to be here, in his own home, amongst his own things—?'

'Perhaps you could both show me around while we talk,' Ms Anderson interrupted. 'I do have to meet the Castellas again soon. I really had no idea, Mr Vanaldi, that you were engaged,' she added as she headed, uninvited, up the stairs.

'Nor did I…' Ainslie muttered, taking Guido in her arms. 'Elijah, what on earth is going on?'

'Just go along with it…' Elijah's voice was low. 'Please.'

'The paternal uncle and aunt naturally want to see Guido…' Ms Anderson said, pausing to frown as she passed the room Ainslie had slept in, her shrewd eyes taking in the backpack on the floor and the noticeably single bed.

'This is your room, Ainslie?'

'Yes,' Ainslie started, then, feeling his hand tighten around hers, realised the trap she'd unwittingly walked into.

'We were not comfortable sleeping in my sister's bed,' Elijah said smoothly. 'So Ainslie suggested she take the room closest to Guido on his first night.'

'And do you have experience with children?'

'She's a kindergarten teacher in Australia.' Elijah smiled like the cat who'd got the cream as he answered for her, and Ms Anderson jotted it down. 'Well, she was until she met me!'

They were in Maria and Rico's room now. Guido was running around and picking up his toys, holding them out to Ainslie and showing her his things.

'Well, it would be nice for Guido to have some consistency during these early days…' Ms Anderson said. 'But the Castellas really—'

'Surely,' Elijah pushed, 'it is better for now that he stays at home—at least for Christmas?'

His blue eyes met Ms Anderson's, and if Ainslie hadn't known better he'd have had her convinced too. He was so assured, so persuasive—and, Ainslie thought with a sudden flurry of nerves, a truly excellent liar!

'If the situation was different I would invite them to stay here. But there is, as I said…' he snapped his fingers as he impatiently summoned suitable words '…bad blood between the families.'

'They have a right to see him.'

'Take him now…' Elijah said easily, but a muscle flickered in his cheek. He thanked his lucky stars for his foresight in hiring Tony for the ease it gave him to make the offer. 'You are meeting with them; let them have some time with Guido. My driver will take you…'

'I can drive myself.'

'His car seat isn't transferable—Tony fitted it this morning—and, given what has just happened, naturally safety is my first concern. Take Guido to see the rest of his family and then—' still he stared at Ms Anderson '—bring my nephew back to his home while the department makes its decision.'

And it sounded reasonable—so reasonable.

Ms Anderson blinked rapidly. 'Do you have help?' She sniffed at the pile of linen still on the bathroom floor.

'Housework was never my sister's forte…' Elijah shrugged. 'She refused to get a housekeeper, and I'm afraid it shows, but I will arrange help in the New Year—there is no chance of getting anyone now.'

'I'll manage…' For the first time since she'd messed up with the sleeping arrangements Ainslie spoke.

'But surely you should be spending time getting to know Guido? This house is huge…' Her eyes swivelled to the next flight of stairs. 'How many levels are there?'

'Four—I have my driver using a room on the third level, but the top is self contained—it would be perfect for a nanny or housekeeper. I'm sure there will be no trouble hiring someone in the New Year.'

'Can I see it?'

'Of course.' Elijah shrugged. 'I will get the keys.' Which took for ever.

When he eventually returned Ainslie was one burning blush, having had to make small talk with an incredibly nosy Ms Anderson. Elijah led them both up the thickly carpeted stairs to the self-contained area.

It was vast—the entire top floor was converted into a three-bedroomed flat, with a huge lounge and tasteful furnishings, but from the thick layer of dust and the cobwebs it must have been closed off for years.

Ms Anderson spoke. 'My sister Enid is actually looking for live-in work—she's extremely qualified…'

'Have her forward her résumé to me,' Elijah said. 'As I said—we'll be looking for someone once we've got this place cleaned up.'

'She's available now.' Her eyes held a challenge as they met Elijah's. 'And I'm sure she'd be happy to clean it to your liking. She's done housekeeping and has childcare qualifications. She's got no family apart from me. Of course you may not want anyone here, getting in the way of you and your lovely new fiancée, but…' Her voice trailed off but her intent was clear, and Elijah met the challenge with a tight smile.

'She sounds perfect.'

'What on earth have you done?' The second Ms Anderson left with Guido, Ainslie confronted him. 'You can't just pass me off as your fiancée!'

'I agree…' Elijah ran a disapproving eye along the length of her body and Ainslie burned with humiliation and anger. 'Hopefully she will think you look such a fright because you got caught in the snow.'

'Well, excuse me!' Ainslie retorted, but her sarcasm was entirely wasted.

'You don't have to apologise. They are not back till four—I can take you shopping…do something with your hair…'

'I'm not talking about how I look,' Ainslie spat, once she'd lifted her jaw from the floor. 'You can't just play around with people's lives like that—you can't just tell me what to do, what to say, what to wear! What on earth made you think I'd say yes!'

'You have no job, no home, and no reference!' Elijah retorted. 'And, as you said to your lover this morning, you like the nice things in life—well, now you get to sample them!'

'How dare you?' Shaking, gibbering with rage, she grabbed an envelope out of her bag, ignoring Elijah's raised eyebrows as she pulled away the wad of notes Angus had given her and thrust the reference under his nose. But Elijah just laughed mirthlessly as he read it.

'I see there is no home number to contact…' His cruel grin widened. 'And so carefully worded too! You know, I admit to knowing nothing about children, but were I considering employing you on the strength of this I would be asking myself why the mother of the children is not so gushing in her praise—why I can only contact the father on his work number…' His eyes challenged her to answer—only Ainslie couldn't. Instead she spoke up.

'You can't railroad me into pretending to be your fiancée.'

'You don't know me.' Elijah shrugged. Maybe he was going about this the wrong way, he conceded to himself. Maybe he should have sat her down, told her just how desperate he was. But panic was taking over at the thought of Guido with the Castellas, of them holding him this very minute, of them *taking* him. And they knew about the house transfer. It all blurred his sentences, until every word, every gesture, was driven by a panic no one must see. 'I can be extremely persuasive when I have to be.'

'I don't mind helping out,' Ainslie retorted. 'I don't mind working for you for a few days…'

'You don't *mind*?' Elijah checked. 'Don't pretend you have options, Ainslie.'

'Oh, but I do…' She wouldn't be spoken to like this. Snatching back her reference, she stuffed it in her bag, then headed up the stairs, taking them two, three at a time. 'I've already booked a place at the youth hostel, and if I can't get another job in the New Year then I'll go back home to Australia.' She was grabbing her clothes, shoving them into her backpack. 'I helped *you* last night, Elijah, not the other way around!' She turned to face him. The heating in the house had brought colour back to her face now, and two angry red spots were burning on her cheeks. 'I might have been in a bit of a pickle, but I'd certainly have managed if you hadn't come along—and, frankly, twelve hours in your company really hasn't changed anything.'

Only it had.

Lugging her backpack down the stairs, Ainslie crashed past the pushchair, the jumble of toys, Maria's and Rico's shoes, and wrenched open the front door. The snow was really falling now. Earls Court Square was pretty in white, but far more attractive-looking through the glass window of a warm house. But anger kept the cold out—anger gave her the strength to somehow drag her backpack and case down the steps and onto the street. And hopefully it would propel her all the way to the youth hostel, away from this pompous, presuming man. Sure, he had problems—and, sure, she felt wretched for Guido. But it wasn't her problem to solve—she already had enough of her own.

'Ainslie.'

The snow seemed to catch the word, seemed to hold it in the air like a snowflake, soaring it, whirring it, circling it, till it landed wintry and lonely on her soul as he walked down the steps to join her.

'You've got staff now—you've got someone to take care of Guido. Your things have arrived, and things are starting to sort themselves out.'

'I am *expected* to have staff!' Elijah retorted. 'If I am to show this woman I am serious about staying here till Guido's future is decided, then I need to have staff!'

'And a fiancée too?'

'Yes!' His voice was urgent. 'Yes, because that woman was two minutes away from deciding I was not suitable. Ainslie, I divide my time between cities, I have properties all over Europe, I fly first class the way most people take a bus. I dine in the best restaurants each night, with the world's most beautiful woman…' And so hopeless was his voice, so abject his misery, Ainslie knew that his impromptu list of credentials had nothing to do with showing off—quite the reverse in this case. 'There are a lot of women who would be only too happy—'

'I get the picture!' Ainslie put up her hand to stop him. She didn't actually want to think about his appalling reputation and the numerous women waiting in the wings. 'If that is your life, Elijah, how on earth do you think you're going to slot in Guido?'

'I don't know.' His honesty touched her. 'I don't know if I am what he needs. I don't even know if that is what I want. From the moment the hospital called me nothing in my world has made sense. All I know is that I have to give it a try. Maria died yesterday, and her last words were that she wanted me to take care of him—if I hand him over to his aunt and uncle now then that will never, ever happen.'

'It won't work.'

'We can make it work,' Elijah insisted. 'If you help me I will help you too. I will give you a reference for anywhere—I don't care if I have to say you worked for me all the time you have been in England…'

'That would be a lie, though.'

'So?' He was standing in front of her in black jeans and a black jumper, his full mouth the only colour in his pale face. Flakes of snow had settled on his black hair and as surly as his response was, she actually understood. This man, who had come out fighting, would continue to fight— because he had everything to lose. 'I need time. Time to think. If it is better for Guido to go with Rico's family, if I see they would be better for him, I will accept that. If adoption is better than the home I can provide, then I will accept that too—but I have to do this for my sister, for Guido, for me. I will lie, I will cheat—I will do whatever it takes. But I ask you to believe my intentions are honourable.'

'I'm not a good liar…' Her teeth were chattering now.

'I can lie for two.'

'And—contrary to what you might think—I don't cheat either.'

He gave just a hint of an ironic smile, his eyebrows raising just a fraction—but, staring down at her, Elijah didn't care if she was actually a very good liar or was just deceiving herself. All that mattered was that she stayed.

'I will pay you well—I will sort out that loan for you.'

It was irrelevant.

As they stood there staring, somehow both knew money wasn't the issue here—that whatever force had first pushed them together was bigger than a pay cheque or a reference.

'If her sister stays—' she was shivering violently now as she spoke '—we're going to have to share a bed...'

'We will put pillows down the middle...' His hands cupped her cheeks, a lazy smile blushing his lips as he eked out the same from her. 'So that you don't take advantage of me.'

He could have kissed her then—it felt as if he *was* kissing her. The caress of his words, his hands on her cheeks, the warmth between them—all defied the bitterness of winter. An outlandish pact was silently made as they stood there—as she glimpsed something, something indefinable, an almost intangible kindness behind that ruthless guarded face. A foretaste of how this man could be. And as he lifted her backpack, and took her case just as easily, and with the other hand held hers and led her up the steps, it was so much more than duty or money or fear that led her back to the house.

It was him.

'Quel sembre volgore!' Drumming his fingers on the couch, not only did Elijah run a bored eye over Ainslie— he spoke over her too.

In the middle of an exclusive London department store he had somehow found what was surely a Milan supermodel masquerading as a shop assistant, and the two of them had absolutely no qualms speaking in Italian and loudly tutting at Ainslie's choice in clothes.

'Vulgar?' Dropping her jaw, Ainslie confronted him. 'Did you just say that I looked vulgar?'

'Those boots!' Elijah flicked his hands at the offending leather. 'And that coat, *would*, at a funeral, look vulgar!'

Staring at the ceiling-to-floor mirrors that showed her from *every* angle, reluctantly Ainslie conceded that he did have a point. The black coat with its nipped-in waist and the long flat leather boots had looked so tasteful, but combined… Well…Ainslie gulped as she caught her reflection from behind—despite being fully dressed, somehow she looked as if she had nothing on underneath.

Unbuttoning the coat with a sigh, for a crazy second she forgot why they were there, forgot the hell of the last twenty-four hours, and forgot where she was, who *he* was. With a cheeky grin Ainslie turned and flashed her fully clothed body at him.

He didn't get the joke.

Ainslie stood as the personal service continued, as a woman dressed like a dental nurse came over and introduced herself as the manager of the beauty salon—only she spoke with Elijah.

Ainslie continued to stand and listen as Elijah told the woman what he wanted to happen with Ainslie's hair.

'I *can* talk!' Ainslie interrupted furiously.

'You don't know what I want done, though.' And he proceeded to dissect her eyebrows, her complexion, openly criticising *everything*, really, as if she were some donkey that needed to be groomed into a glossy racehorse.

'What about the clothes?'

'I'll take care of that with Tania,' Elijah answered, 'now we've worked out what *doesn't* suit you! And despite what she might say to you, my fiancée does *not* just need a trim!' Elijah flashed Ainslie a quick warning smile as he spoke with the manager. 'She needs it properly cut and styled—and please…' He held up a wad of curls and examined the rather sun-bleached ends. 'Can you do something with the colour too?'

She was determined to hate it!

She sat bristling with anger as her eyebrows were waxed, a face mask was applied, along with a hair dye, and her finger and toenails were simultaneously pummelled and painted—as half the salon set to work to transform her into a woman deemed worthy enough to wear his cheap ring.

'The colour's marvellous!' The chief colourist beamed at the final unveiling. 'It really suits you.'

Her naturally honey-blonde hair, which had spent way too long in the ocean and being dried by the harsh Australian sun, was now a much softer ash-blonde. The cut was just superb and, despite her best efforts not to, Ainslie couldn't help but lean forward in her chair, pulling at one heavy curl and blinking her newly dyed lashes as it popped back into perfect shape beside a perfect eyebrow. As the make-up therapist pointed out, the dark grey eyeshadow and charcoal liner really *did* bring out the green of her eyes—and what was more, Ainslie realised, sucking in her lips, contrary to what she'd previously thought she *did* have cheekbones!

'That's better!' Elijah barely glanced up from the newspaper he was reading as she came out of the salon.

'I pass, do I?' Ainslie retorted. But as always the last word went to Elijah.

'Once you get some decent clothes on.'

And, loathsome as he was, he was right. In soft grey wool trousers, topped with the palest pink jumper which felt as blissful to touch as it was to wear, sitting in the lounge as they awaited Tony and Guido's arrival, she felt horribly awkward, but really rather good.

Ainslie was appalled when Elijah caught her peering in her compact mirror, flicking back her hair, but he didn't comment, just stared moodily out of the window till the rest of his waifs and strays arrived. Ainslie joined him to watch as they all spilled out of the car. Ms Anderson, carrying Guido, who was closely followed by a woman who must be her sister—and Tony, an absolute brute of a man, his chauffeur uniform way too tight for his huge frame, taking up the rear.

'I should put up a sign to tell people I've had a change of career...' Elijah sighed, and despite herself Ainslie giggled. 'Let everyone know that I'm running a refuge for the homeless and displaced.'

Enid was nothing, *nothing* like her rather prim sister.

With a booming Northern accent she introduced herself, ruffled Guido's hair and then headed for the kitchen.

'Would you like me to show you your accommodation?' Ainslie offered.

'I'm sure I'll find it!'

'Or a cup of coffee, perhaps?'

'I'll bring you one through in just a moment.'

Elijah just laughed at her burning blush when Enid stalked off to the kitchen.

'I was offering to make *her* one!'

'Then don't.' He grinned. 'Remember your place—and that is up here, with me!'

Loathsome snob, Ainslie thought, but didn't say it.

As Tony dragged suitcase after suitcase up the stairs, assuring Elijah he'd soon be out of their way, Enid button-holed Ainslie and asked to be taken through her routine.

'We don't actually have much of a routine.'

Ainslie's eyes darted to Elijah, who was too busy playing with a grizzling Guido to notice.

'I understand you haven't established one with Guido yet,' Enid said kindly. 'I was talking more about meals, what sort of things you and Mr Vanaldi like to eat.'

'We tend to dine out, though obviously we won't be as much now…' Ainslie said helplessly, praying he wasn't allergic to nuts or had celiac disease or something dire. 'Anything, really!'

'I'm quite a plain cook,' Enid warned her, standing up. 'And there's not much in the kitchen. I'll see what I can manage to rustle up for tonight.'

'This is like a nightmare,' Ainslie whispered when she'd gone. 'I don't even know how many sugars you have in your coffee.'

'Three.' Elijah shrugged, watching as Guido stood on two fat legs and tottered over to Ainslie, holding his arms out to be lifted, which she did. Scooping him up in her arms and instead of, as she had been, trying to cheer him, she calmed him down, pulled him right into her and stroked his hair, soothed him with assurances after, Elijah realised then, what must have been another daunting day for Guido—meeting strangers, missing his parents.

'You're good with him.'

'It's my—' Ainslie started, but didn't finish. And it wasn't because Enid came back into the room that her voice trailed off. Holding Guido, feeling him relax against her, Ainslie knew in her heart that this was so much more than a job.

Bravely, Ainslie thought, Enid had made spaghetti bolognaise for her and Elijah. But he simply fell on it. He mopped his plate with bread when he'd finished, then proceeded to tell her the plans for the funeral.

'It was either Christmas Eve, or wait another week.'

'What would you prefer?'

'Neither…' Elijah admitted. 'But I chose Christmas Eve. It's going to be hell either way, and I think it is better we get it over with, then do our best for Guido on Christmas Day.'

'What did Rico's family want?'

'To know who was paying for it. Naturally Ms Anderson tried to rephrase it, but that was their main concern. I've booked a hotel for afterwards, and I've rung all the friends in Maria's diary and replied to a few of her e-mails. One of the mothers from Guido's playgroup rang by chance today, to speak with Maria…' He faltered for just a second. 'She had no idea what had happened.'

'That must have been awful for you.'

'I would prefer it if you didn't answer the house phone. I will tell Enid also. I don't want to put either of you through it. I ended up consoling her…' He buried his face in his hands, the sarcasm, the jibes, the whole mask slipping as he let out a low rumble of a moan. 'This is so wrong—it just all is so wrong. Like a mistake has been made.'

'It has!' Ainslie could hear his pain, feel it from across the table.

'I went to ring her earlier.' He looked up, strong features

now hopeless. 'I went to dial this number—to ask her what flowers she liked… That is crazy…'

'It's not crazy…' She couldn't just sit and watch him sink. On reflex she went over to him, stood where he sat, rested her hands on his strained shoulders. 'You're not crazy—it's normal, I'm sure.'

'I want to ask her what I should do…' His anguish was there in each word, beneath her fingers his shoulders were rigid in her hands. 'I want to know what she would want.'

She could see her own fingers, pale against his black jumper, digging in and massaging the knots of tension, could see them moving against her will, as if they belonged to someone else. Instinctively her hands moved, working each taut bundle of tension till she felt the release.

'She already told you what she wanted.'

He nodded, taking solace in her words, taking solace in her touch—only for both of them it wasn't over. She was aware now that she was touching him. Some bizarre out-of-body experience had seen her cross the room, only now her mind was back, registering the change of surrounds and her fingers that had worked his flesh so easily were moving clumsily now…she jerked away when Enid came in the room.

'Ainslie…?' The question in Elijah's voice faded as he saw they had company.

'Don't mind me!' The housekeeper smiled, taking the plates as, awkward, blushing, Ainslie stepped back.

But later, lying in the bath, staring at the still water as she lay motionless, Ainslie knew her blushes, her awkwardness, had had nothing to do with Enid entering. It had been the contact that had her reeling—her own boldness, her own *knowing*, which had propelled her like iron ore to a magnet. And it wasn't a question of pleasing, Ainslie realised as still she lay. It wasn't a question of being good enough. It was knowing that you were.

That with him, kissing him, touching him, it wasn't about Elijah's skill or experience, or any of the stuff she'd read about as she'd muddled through the maze of dating.

It all came down to *her* and how he made her feel—the woman he brought out in her.

And now they had to share a bed.

CHAPTER SIX

'OH, PLEASE no!' Pulling acres of purple satin out of tissue paper, Ainslie stared at him aghast as she held up the offending garments. 'Do men actually like this stuff?'

'Tell me what I should have said!' Elijah snapped from his vantage point on the bed, a wad of pillows dividing the battlefield. 'Should I have told the assistant who was selecting your wardrobe that this particular billionaire's fiancée actually prefers flannelette pyjamas that are covered in monkeys?'

'I'm not wearing this!'

'Fine!' Elijah snapped. 'I'm sure Enid has seen naked ladies in the hallway at midnight; she probably won't turn a hair. I am telling you—you are not wearing those pyjamas.'

'I am!'

'Actually, you can't!' Elijah sniped as she unzipped her backpack. 'Because I threw out all your tat!'

He had!

'Don't you *ever* go through my things again!'

'That's a fine thing to say—given your current circumstances!'

He did feel a twinge of unfamiliar guilt as she flounced

out. Today had been hard for her too, and he had seen the flash of tears in eyes as she'd raced for the door—but, hell, what did she expect? Elijah consoled himself. If they were going to pass her off as his fiancée she could hardly walk around in high street clothes and fake handbags!

She was a funny little thing, though. Despite his hell, Elijah found himself smiling inside when she returned from the bathroom, her skin clashing violently with the satin and her whole body one burning blush. Despite the fact that this man actually *didn't* like that sort of stuff, he felt a stirring beneath the sheet that said otherwise. He couldn't help but notice the unfamiliar sight of a round bottom and the curve of a stomach the nightdress clung to—such a contrast to the reed-thin women he was used to bedding—and he couldn't help but notice a glimpse of pink areola as she leant to pull back the covers. What she lacked in sophistication she repaid tenfold in femininity. She slipped into bed beside him, then slid halfway down the sheets—a waft of toothpaste the only scent to greet him. Never had spearmint been more refreshing… Or, Elijah thought, hands bunched into fists above the sheet, never had the scent of spearmint been more sexy!

He could feel her twitching with nerves beside him, feel her vulnerability, and it moved him—he knew she was expecting him to pounce. But that would only complicate things. He'd assured her there would be no repeats.

'Goodnight!' he barked, flicking off the light, willing himself to sleep. But every time he closed his eyes all he could see was her. Not the image of her tonight, or even today. Instead the image of her last night was the one that danced before his eyes, the feel her in his arms, the soft balmy escape of her lips.

No repeats.

Blowing out his breath, he willed sleep to come, but knew it would evade him. He resigned himself instead to a long, sleepless night.

Ainslie wasn't faring much better. Staring into the sudden darkness, she felt her throat so constricted, her body so rigid, that she couldn't attempt to answer his brusque goodnight.

In the sexiest lingerie, next to the sexiest man, all she felt was stupid. The whole day had been one awful lesson in humiliation. And, lest she forget, she recalled him at the department store, holding up her hair as if it were a rag, replayed over and over in her mind every sarcastic barb he had uttered. The fact that he was lying utterly unmoved beside her reinforced that she was nowhere near the type of woman Elijah Vanaldi dated.

So why had he kissed her?

Her blush was back. She stared unseeing at the ceiling as she felt him restless beside her, his uneven breathing telling her that he wasn't asleep.

And thank God for the pillows between them—because just at the memory of his kiss she wanted to curl towards him. Her whole body seemed to be leaping like a salmon in an autumn river—defying her wishes to settle and heading upstream as Elijah blew out a breath beside her.

He had kissed her because he could, Ainslie decided. Because his sister had just died and she had been there.

She could feel her hands on his shoulders again, feel the velvet of his skin as she'd stroked his neck, the bit of flesh at the nape of his neck she'd wanted to lower her head to and kiss…

She breathed out into the darkness. The air was so thick, so warm, it was an effort to drag a breath back in. Her skin was too warm from the bath, the covers a heavy weight as Elijah lay restless beside her.

'I'm sorry—I need to go to the loo!' Her voice was a croak as, with an almost weary sigh, Elijah reached over and switched the light back on. 'It's static…' A slightly hysterical giggle wobbled in her throat as she slid off the sheet and peeled the nightdress from her body. Her hair crackled as it left the pillow 'It's ruining my hair!'

He didn't even deign to smile.

God, she looked a sight.

Staring in the mirror at her hair sticking up everywhere, and her flesh spilling out, Ainslie was about to tuck one wayward bosom back safely into her nightdress when Elijah came in behind her. Such was the blaze in his eyes, so heavy was her want, she didn't even pretend to scold him for not knocking.

'I would never have chosen this for you to wear.'

His hand caught hers, cupping her breast, and she watched in the mirror as he lowered his noble head to her neck, as he kissed her there deeply. Her own hand slipped, leaving his, and she watched with morbid fascination as her nipple lengthened, a whimper of regret escaping as he released her. All Ainslie knew was that she couldn't even try to fight it any more. The attraction, the intent, the presence that was there between them was just so overwhelming, so intense, it was as impossible to fathom as it was to ignore. She couldn't breathe—or rather, she could—but they were rapid shallow breaths that made her dizzy.

Standing frozen, watching in the mirror as he turned on the shower, she closed her eyes with giddy excitement as he returned a second later and led her, thousand-dollar nightdress and all, under the jets. The bliss of the water as it hit her stiff lacquered hair made her shiver. Wet satin clung to her as he poured shampoo and massaged it into her scalp, as his tongue stroked hers and his hands pulled at the fabric, pushing it down over her body, pressing her with his own body against the cold glass.

He was naked now too—and though she'd seen most of him, she hadn't seen this bit of him, and her equanimity was dimmed for ever as he revealed the splendid, terrifying sight of himself in full arousal. Whether from reflex or awe her knees went weak. She sank to the floor of the shower, kissing him intimately, tasting the soapy, wet maleness of him as the water kissed her eyes, as his fingers knotted in her hair—till he stopped her, till he held her face in the palm of his hands and forced her head up.

'This is how I want you…' Bedraggled, soaked, her eyes glittering with desire, face flushed despite the cool water, and utterly, utterly drunk on lust, he took in her every feature, then dragged her to her feet before he spoke again. '*This* is how you come to me at night.'

Impatient fingers were parting her thighs now, and his mouth was hungry at her breast, sucking, bruising, biting. It was delicious—as delicious as the hot pulse between her legs, beating for his fierce erection. Like a locating device he sought her. She could see him, full to bursting, wondered if he'd make it, if she'd make it, and was grateful his haste matched hers when he slipped inside her. Her orgasm was so deep, so intense, it made her sob with its power.

Everything dimmed as they centred, as for a minute she was lost to everything but him. Then came a dim awareness of her surrounds, and the cool water brought her round to a world that was different. Sensations were sharper somehow, the water too cool on her body, too loud in her ears. It must have been for him too, because Elijah turned off the taps, wrapped her in a towel and, placing another one around his hips, led her back to bed.

It was like getting up the first time after the flu—her legs weak, her body shivering, drained from the exertion, thrilled to be up but ready to slip back into bed.

But not till he'd dried her—and not just her skin, but her hair too. Then he pulled back the covers, and she lay there.

'Can we get rid of the safety barrier now?' He pulled the pillows away, but she couldn't smile, couldn't look at him—trying to make sense of a world that was the same only different from the one she'd left for a little while. She turned away from him.

'Don't run away from me as well.'

'I'm not.' His fingers traced the length of her spine, then over her bottom, tracing her contours, soothing her body as she struggled with her mind. 'I didn't.'

And she *hadn't* been running away, coming to London. She hadn't been walking out on her life. But she had been searching. Not for him, but for the bit of her that was missing—the something she had never been able to define but that she'd glimpsed tonight.

The wantonness he'd unleashed, this passion that had been untapped—it wasn't just sex. For her, at least…

'Look at me, then.' So easily he turned her over, and so hard was it to look at him.

'Have you any idea what you've done for me? Without you here I would be in hell—and instead…'

She could look at him now, could see the certainty in his eyes that chased away her doubts. This was as good and as right and as *necessary* as it had felt. In his arms she could feel the thick rope of connection that ran between them, that told her it was so much more than sex that had led her to his bed, that made her dizzy lying in his arms. His beauty astonished her—mesmerised her now that she could face him—and his words told her it was all okay, that she was safe to be the woman she was with him.

He confirmed it with a kiss. It was supremely tender, a long, languorous kiss now that the urgency was gone—a kiss to taste him, to explore him, and he let her take her time to relish in it. The need that had gripped them before was replaced now by a deeper want—a want to touch him, to allow her fingers, her mouth, to grow familiar with him, tracing his image with her senses, taking in details, like the swirl of hair around his areolae, the soapy taste of his flat hard nipple in her mouth, his moans as she licked it.

He explored her too, curves that he had once felt too generous entirely in proportion now as he revelled in her body. His pleasure was rising in her hands as he suckled her. A knot of legs as he entered her, and side on they faced each other. For the first time she didn't close her eyes, and neither did he, and she could have stayed like that for ever. Elijah was in no rush. His length was inside her and his eyes adored her. Rocking together, just locked in an unhurried pleasure. Relishing the slide of skin on skin and the delicious friction they created—hardly moving on the outside, but long, slow strokes stirred her deep within.

Each touch, each caress answered an unvoiced plea. She'd found her soul mate, like some glorious dance in the mirror, he echoed her thoughts and answered her wants.

It was a dance that couldn't go on for ever because the tip to transition had her crying, had him calling out her name as he filled her with his gift.

'Don't leave me.'

He groaned it out as he spilled inside her, and she dragged him in deeper in answer, so sure at that moment, so utterly and completely sure, that she never would.

CHAPTER SEVEN

'GUIDO, ritornato qui!'

But not even Elijah's stern order for Guido to come back could halt him. Giggling, running along the landing, Ainslie was awoken to the missile of a cheeky pre-dawn toddler, wide awake and ready to play, launching himself onto the bed as his exasperated uncle ran behind, just as he had the last few mornings. A strange glow of a routine, that was theirs, was forming out of the chaos.

'He escaped again!' Elijah explained, taking two kicking legs and trying to assert some authority *and* put on a nappy. But Guido, slippery with nappy cream, wriggled out of his strong hands, laughing and coughing and running across the bed to a grinning Ainslie.

'Here,' Ainslie offered, taking the nappy and tickling Guido on the tummy, making him laugh by blowing raspberries on his feet and managing to get his fat slippery body into the nappy as Elijah stretched out on the bed beside them, exhausted from his morning exercise with Guido.

'How can one person who is so small create so much chaos?'

'Very easily,' Ainslie grinned. 'They can smell fear too, you know.'

For a second he was about to refute her—Ainslie actually felt his body stiffen beside her, just as it had when she had first offered help—but then he laughed. This closed, guarded, stern man, who had so much on his mind, actually threw his head back and laughed. 'He terrifies me!'

And when Elijah laughed Guido did too, absolutely sensing weakness and crawling over the bed to his uncle, sitting on his chest and pressing fat hands into his face.

'You are trouble…' Elijah scowled to his delighted audience. 'Should we keep you?'

It sounded like the worst thing to say—so utterly open to misinterpretation that even Ainslie was jolted for a second—but lying there beside him, with Guido bouncing up and down, it was the nicest thing he could possibly have said.

Normal, almost.

Just the sort of thing one might say with absolute confidence because the answer wasn't in question—the sort of thing a parent might say to a child in all the certainty it was loved.

And he was.

'Always I tell Maria she is not strict enough with him.' He was holding Guido's hands now, and pulling him up to stand on his chest. 'She had no routine. I would come from the airport sometimes at ten at night and he would be still up playing—she couldn't say no to him… I tell her: that boy will be trouble…' He gave a wry smile. 'Had I known she was leaving the trouble for me, I would have insisted she was stricter.'

All of it he said with mirth, not a trace of pity, as Guido

played trampoline on his chest. But Elijah's words were so bittersweet they brought the sting of tears to Ainslie's eyes, as she watched this man who knew nothing about babies doing so very, very well—saw the genuine affection between uncle and nephew, the humour and history that bound families as the two of them became one. The ties that loosely bound them were tightening as she watched on—only it wasn't duty or obligation that was pulling the strings. There in the bed, sharing the dawn, Guido and his uncle were starting to become a family.

And—even if by default—Ainslie was a part of it too. She was scarcely able to comprehend that their chance encounter had been more than a meeting of minds, but bodies and souls too—that the passion that still taunted her with its recklessness, when she had a moment alone to dwell, made absolute sense when it was just the two of them…or three.

She'd worked with children since she was eighteen—had had her favourites too—but never had one captured her heart like Guido. It wasn't just his plight—the children in her care had had their traumas too—it was Guido's spirit that melted her. His eyes once as blue and as mistrusting as his uncle's that suddenly adored her when they smiled.

He was smiling at her now. Tired of being naughty, Guido had slid down his uncle's chest as the grown-ups planned his day, his thick lashes getting heavier by the minute as he lay between them, thumb in mouth, smiling lazily.

'He is still coughing.' Elijah frowned down in concern as Guido gave a croupy bark.

'Not as much…' Ainslie stroked the little dark curls. 'And croup can last for ages—he seems much better.'

'Still, maybe he should stay here today—it is the funeral

tomorrow…' Guido was supposed to be going to the Castellas for the afternoon. Ms Anderson had made it quite clear that regular contact was to be maintained with the Castellas while the Social Services department made its decision. Ainslie had pointed out on numerous occasions that it could only help Elijah's case if he showed willing, yet still he resisted. 'I will ring Ms Anderson—explain to her that—'

'You need to let him go,' Ainslie said softly. 'He'll be in a warm car, and Enid will be with him—there's no reason for him not to go.'

'Oh, but there is.' He was staring down at his nephew, his face colourless in the wintry dawn light as a chink in the curtain let in a grey slice of morning. The frost on the glass warned that it was cold outside, but it was so warm in here. 'Here—with me, with us—I know he is safe.'

He was. Little Guido, warm and asleep now between them, dreaming milky dreams and without a care in the world, was safe in the knowledge that he was loved, innocently trusting those who looked after him—and though Ainslie could see why Elijah didn't want to let him go, she also knew that he had to.

Despite their intimacy, Elijah's grief was his own—a private place she rarely glimpsed. His pain, his mistrust, the weight of the decisions he must soon make, were things he chose to explore alone, but there was no place as comfortable as the morning bed for exploring options. Bodies relaxed and minds refreshed from sleep, open to the gifts of a new day, brought a closeness, an ease, and for the first time they explored their new territory.

'Guido needs his family. Even if you don't like them, they are still his family. Maybe you have to try to put the past aside, for Guido's sake.' She watched his eyes shutter, watched his face actually grimace in resistance to her words, but instead of a clipped refusal to even listen to her reasoning, Elijah actually struggled to grasp it.

'Everything in me tells me not to trust them—that they are no good…' His eyes found hers then, and for once they were lost. 'I survive not just because I am clever but on *istinto*—on instinct. Now everyone tells me I am to ignore the thing that has kept me alive, that I must trust Guido to these people when it goes against everything I feel.'

'People do change, Elijah. What happened with Maria was years ago. I'm not making excuses—I'm not!' she said quickly again, when he opened his mouth to argue. 'I just think for Guido's sake you have to show good faith—you have to trust that his uncle and aunt want what's best for him too, even if it's hard for you to see it. Ringing Ms Anderson and making excuses, suggesting they might have had something to do with the accident—well, it's just making you look…' She didn't finish, just lay there staring over at him.

His head on the pillow, he was staring up at the ceiling, seemingly not listening. But he was. Racked with indecision, he lay there—he could feel the rise and fall of Guido's chest against his arm. His sister's most treasured possession. One she had entrusted him to take care of, to do his best for. And every fibre of his being told him to keep Guido by his side, that two minutes in the Castellas' company was two minutes too long. Yet his instinct had told him Ainslie wasn't a thief, intuition had told him he could trust her—and here she was, without agenda, telling him to let Guido go to the enemy, that everything would be okay…

Snapping his face to hers, Elijah surprised her with a smile as he finished her sentence for her.

'I look bitter?' he offered. 'Paranoid, even?'

'Just a bit.' Ainslie grinned. Suddenly he didn't look either of the two. The man smiling back looked ten years younger than the one she had first met. 'Do you want me to put Guido back in his cot?'

'Why?' Elijah asked, lids closing on his blue eyes, pulling his nephew into the crook of his arm and toying with Ainslie's hair.

She watched as he drifted off, watched for the first time this suspicious, mistrusting man actually relax. Only now it was Ainslie who couldn't.

He had listened to her.

The two men who had suddenly become so vital in her life both trusted her.

She just hoped she was saying the right thing.

'They've been gone too long.'

'It's only six…' Ainslie glanced at the clock on the mantelpiece for, oh, maybe the hundredth time. They'd had a busy day—first going to the undertakers, where Elijah had grimly gone through the difficult task of making the final preparations for tomorrow, then, taking a welcome pause from frantic last-minute Christmas shopping, Elijah had suggested somewhere nice for a late lunch.

'We'll never get a table there,' Ainslie had warned. 'Not at this time of year!'

Elijah had just frowned and pulled out his phone, and whatever the abracadabra word was that conjured up a table out of nowhere for the rich and the beautiful, some-where in Italy his PA must have uttered it, because they had bypassed the grumbling queue, hadn't even been led to the bar! The beaming *maître d'* had greeted them by name and led them to a secluded table where a leisurely lunch had been taken.

Then they had parted for a couple of hours and hit the mad crowds. As busy and as crazy as the crowds had been, it *felt* like Christmas, carols blasting from record shops and brass bands adding to the seasonal feel.

Ainslie still found it hard to fathom that the sun set so early in England, but she was so glad it did. The gloomy af-ternoon had been giving way to dusk and the whole of Oxford Street was a canopy of lights, more magical and ex-travagant than she could have imagined, as she'd met up with Elijah and they'd jumped in a black taxi to head for home.

Only now it wasn't just the light of the day that had faded fast, but Elijah's easy mood as he waited for his nephew to return. 'I will ring Enid....' He was pulling his phone out of his pocket when the car pulled up. But the tension that had abated only slightly with their arrival returned as Guido, grizzling and miserable, entered the house. Enid was tight-lipped as she took off her coat, while Ainslie did the same for Guido.

'It's been a long day for him,' Enid said. 'I'll go and get him some dinner.'

'It's after six,' Elijah pointed out. 'Did they not give him any dinner?'

'They eat late.' Enid answered carefully, but Elijah was having none of it, and demanded to know what the problem was.

Enid remained tight-lipped. 'I don't want to make things any worse than they are.' Enid glanced to Ainslie for support. 'Nothing actually happened. They just weren't as friendly with him this time…'

'When your sister wasn't present,' Elijah pointed out.

'They don't know she's my sister…' Enid started, then her voice trailed off. 'It was just a difficult day. They were talking in Italian, and I didn't feel very welcome, that's all. Not that I'm complaining—it's important Guido sees his family…'

'Where was Tony?'

'Waiting outside in the car,' Enid huffed. 'They never even took him out a drink.'

'He comes in with you next time,' Elijah said. 'And if they have any problems with that, they can discuss it with me.'

'It's not necessary.' Enid shook her head. 'They were no doubt just upset—they're burying one of their family tomorrow too. It's a tense time for everyone.' She handed him an envelope. 'They asked me to give you this.'

Elijah face was black as thunder as he opened it. 'Their accommodation bill.' His lip sneered in distaste. 'It is clear they are after his money. You tell your sister—'

'I don't gossip to my sister about work.' Enid fixed him with a stern glare. 'If the Social Services department formally asks me, then of course I'll give my opinion. But I won't be running to my sister with every bit of gossip about the Castellas the same way I wouldn't discuss *your* dealings—you're my employer. Now, if you'll excuse me, I'm going to give Guido his supper.'

'Where does that leave me?' Elijah asked once they were alone. 'Even if she did put it in a formal report, Social Services would just disregard it.'

'There's nothing to *put* in a formal report,' Ainslie pointed out. 'Elijah, they're allowed to be upset and distracted today—they didn't do anything wrong.'

'Why would you be on their side?' His eyes flashed angrily. 'Guido comes home upset, having been ignored all day, and they send me the bill for their accommodation with a note saying that was it not for me they wouldn't be here... *Zingareschi!*' From the murderous look on Elijah's face as he tossed the note across the room, he hadn't just uttered a compliment! 'The peasants can't even spell in their own language.'

'Elijah, who is this helping?' Ainslie just wouldn't have it—refused to lose what they had found that morning. Walking over, she stood before him, stared up at his face, twisted and bitter with hate, and placed her hand on his cheek. 'You have to be the reasonable one here, for Guido's sake. Maybe they genuinely can't afford the accommodation...'

'So they expect *me* to pay? What is reasonable about that?'

'They're Guido's family—and if you can help now, who knows...?' She was loath to suggest it, but brave enough to do so. 'Elijah, what if they do end up with custody? Or what if you end up with shared care...?'

'No! I won't let it happen.'

'But it might!' Ainslie insisted. 'And anything you can do to forge a relationship with them now can surely only help Guido.'

'Even if it goes against everything I believe?'

He didn't get it, but she could see him struggling, could feel him wrestle with a hatred that was inbred, for the sake of his nephew.

There was nothing more honourable than what he did, this proud, strong man, after a moment's deep thought, nodded, actually backing down. 'I will try,' Elijah said. 'Tomorrow—I will try.'

CHAPTER EIGHT

NOT on Christmas Eve.

Standing in the cemetery, for a crazy second Ainslie wanted to shout it out. Tell the priest to stop.

Because someone somewhere had surely got it wrong?

Christmas was about love and laughter and magic. Not this—never this.

The coroner had released the bodies, and, as Elijah had wearily conceded, it was either today or wait till after the festivities—delay the agony a while longer.

She couldn't fathom his pain.

Couldn't fathom it because even though she'd never met them, as she watched two coffins being lowered into the ground, saw the dark mound of earth that would cover them rising out of the snow, heard Guido innocently sing and chatter to the shell-shocked gathering, Ainslie was overwhelmed with the horror of it all.

She understood exactly what Elijah had said—it was as if a terrible mistake had been made, as if the universe had, on this occasion, got it terribly, terribly wrong.

Yet somehow he held it together—as he had over the last few days, as he had during the service—his deep low voice breaking just once as he'd delivered the eulogy. Returning to her side afterwards he'd sat rigid, staring ahead, somehow doing what had to be done, getting through this most vile of days.

And she wanted to comfort, to offer support, but he neither sought nor accepted it. The hand that she had slipped into his when he came back to his seat had been quickly returned to her own lap unheld—and now, seemingly together but utterly apart, they stood at the graveside as the burial was concluded.

'I will talk to them now.' Holding Guido, instructing her to wait there, he made his way over to the Castellas—to the people he hadn't seen in years but had hated from a distance.

Ainslie's heart was in her mouth.

'How are things?' Ms Anderson was watching too.

'Difficult,' Ainslie admitted. 'But Elijah is making an effort.'

'As he should,' she said tartly. 'The Castellas are Guido's family too.'

But Elijah wasn't up to performing for the cameras, or rather for Ms Anderson. After the briefest of conversations he turned away, his black coat like a cloak billowing behind as he quickly marched. His face was a mask of rigid muscles as he reached Ainslie and Ms Anderson.

'Let's go.'

'You're supposed to—' Ainslie started, but he was already gone.

The undertaker was forming relatives into a line, on the premise that the mourners could shake their hands, or kiss as was the Italian way, and offer their condolences, but Elijah was having none of it.

'Come on!' he called over his shoulder.

'We can't…' He was in no mood to be argued with, but Ainslie tried. 'You're expected to line up—people want to see Guido.'

'They've seen enough!' Elijah retorted, stalking off. 'He's seen enough! I do not need their condolences!'

'That must have been extremely hard for you!' Speaking in her best social worker voice, but slightly breathless, Ms Anderson caught up with them as they reached the car. But Elijah clearly had more on his mind than winning favour with the social worker, because he didn't even deign to give a response. 'The Castellas are looking forward to spending some time with Guido back at the hotel.'

'He won't be there,' Elijah growled, his jaw tightening as the Castellas came over—and for the first time Ainslie saw the two families together, felt the simmering hatred.

'Mr Vanaldi isn't bringing Guido back to the hotel.' Ms Anderson's clipped voice was in stark contrast to the emotive protests of the Castellas.

'Voglio passare tempo con Guido.' Marco Castella put out his hands to his nephew, who clung tighter to Elijah.

'Non potere,' Elijah answered tightly.

'Voglio specialmente oggi essere con lui.'

'Would you mind telling me what's being said.'

Less than impressed, Ms Anderson confronted Elijah. Very much less than intimidated, he gave a surly translation.

'They say they want to spend some time with Guido. I tell them they can't.'

'Today—*specialmente*…' Marco's English was broken, his voice too as he pleaded to Ms Anderson for some time with his nephew. 'We are family.'

And no matter the bad blood between them, no matter that it was Elijah's side she should be on, Ainslie thought that Marco was right—a lavish spread had been put on at a luxury hotel. Surely it was right that Guido go along.

'Maybe we should bring him for a short while…'

Ainslie's suggestion was met with the filthiest of glares.

'Absolutely,' Ms Anderson flared. 'Mr Vanaldi—you have been granted *temporary* access only. Now, I shouldn't have to point out—'

'Then don't,' Elijah broke in, his eyes flashing angrily. 'Over and over you tell me that the best interests of the child are to be considered, that Guido must come first.'

'Of course!'

'You are the expert,' Elijah spat the words at the woman. 'So tell me, Ms Anderson, how Guido's interests are best to be served? My sister refused morphine in order to be able to tell me that he sleeps at two p.m. each afternoon. My nephew is recovering from a serious ear infection and croup, and his whole world has been turned around. How is it better that he goes to a hotel, where people will be drinking, where people will be emotional? Please—tell me now how it would be in his best interests to attend?'

She couldn't. Just stood rigid as Elijah awaited her response. But Guido was on his uncle's side, managing a timely croupy cough that broke the appalling silence.

'Quite!' Elijah said tartly. 'I will take my nephew home now—I will give him his antibiotic and settle him for his afternoon sleep. And when he is settled, my housekeeper— *with* childcare qualifications—will watch him for a couple of hours while my fiancée and I attend this circus.' He nodded to Tony, who opened the car door, and despite his anger, despite his palpable fury, Elijah was supremely gentle as he placed Guido in his car seat. Once they were all in, he wound down the window, his breath white as he hissed out his parting shot, pulling out an envelope from the glove box and thrusting it to Ms Anderson. 'The Castellas want their accommodation bill settled—I trust your department will take care of that?'

'You're right.' As Tony sped them home, it was Ainslie who finally spoke.

'I'm always right.'

'But…' Ainslie chewed her lip for a moment before continuing. 'If you want to appear the better option for Guido, surely it's better that you don't put Ms Anderson off side? I mean, perhaps you should try…'

'I *am* the better option, compared to them,' Elijah retorted. 'I do not need to *try* for anyone.'

'Then why am I here?' Ainslie snapped back. 'Appearances *do* matter!' She snapped her mouth closed, remembering that Tony was present, realising that this conversation couldn't take place here. But it would seem Elijah was past caring, all pretences dropped as he glared back at her and spat out his response.

'You are here because without a rapid fiancée I would not have been able to prevent them from taking him. Now I have time to properly sort out this mess—and I will sort it out! You are paid to appear supportive—remember that next time you contradict me in front of the social worker.'

If he didn't care that Tony was present, then neither did she. 'Am I paid to sleep with you too?'

'No—that's a privilege!'

If he hadn't been right in what he'd said to Ms

Anderson, she'd have told Tony to stop the car so she could get out. If it hadn't been his sister's funeral today, and if Guido hadn't been present, she'd have slapped his cheek. She had to settle for words instead.

'You bastard!'

'Consider it a perk of your job!' Elijah reiterated as they pulled up at the house.

Just in case she hadn't got the point. Just in case he hadn't humiliated her enough.

'How was it?' Enid's kind concern went unanswered as Elijah marched through the hall, the massive house a shrunken vacuum as tension consumed it.

Ainslie sat on the edge of the sofa, too stunned, too angry, too shocked to even *think* about acting normal.

But it seemed Elijah still could. He took the lunch Enid had prepared for Guido and fed the little boy, the vileness that had been on his lips absent as he spoke gently to his nephew. He shook his head at the cup of tea Enid proffered, while still Ainslie sat—ready to leave. Because how, *how*, after that, could she possibly stay?

'Let me put him to bed for you,' Enid offered.

'I'll manage,' Elijah answered, almost in a growl.

'This must be so hard for him…' Enid said as she sat on the couch beside Ainslie. 'For you too.'

And for a second Ainslie felt guilty. Enid's sympathy was utterly unmerited, given the charade they'd created, but tears stung the back of her eyes. The pain the day had inflicted was so raw, his words had been so acutely painful, it was enough to propel her from the sofa, to make a stand, to leave. But, hearing the slam of the bathroom door, hearing Elijah retch, hearing the spasms of pain that engulfed him, hearing some of the hell he held inside, she was overwhelmed too. Her own stomach tightened—doubling over, she sat back down, tears spilling out as she heard the depth of his grief—knowing, knowing at some level the pain he'd inflicted hadn't been aimed at her—yet he'd been too angry, too raw, just too detestable to pardon.

'We should go.' Grey, remote, and utterly not meeting her eyes, Elijah came into the lounge. 'Enid, you are to call if there is a problem.'

'Of course.'

'Come!' He summoned her, heading for the door, clearly expecting Ainslie to follow—only she couldn't. Couldn't just get up and meekly follow, no matter how much he was paying her.

'You really expect me to stand there and play—?'

'Would you excuse us, please, Enid?' he interrupted. 'It would seem my fiancée has something she wants to get off her chest.'

'Why bother?' Ainslie said when the door had closed behind her. 'Why get rid of Enid when we know Tony's going to tell her? There's no point pretending any more.'

'Tony won't tell her.'

'Of course he will!' Ainslie scorned.

'I employ Tony—he knows what is expected from him. I pay for his discretion!'

'Pay for him to sit quiet while you dare to speak to me like that?' Ainslie spat. 'Well, even a fake fiancée doesn't have to put up with that.' She was pulling at his ring. The sudden heat of the house after the cold outside made it hard to get it off, giving Elijah the second it took to cross the room and close his hands around hers—only it wasn't in apology.

'You will come with me this afternoon.'

'Or?' Ainslie challenged. 'You don't own me—I'll pay my own debts, Elijah, my ex's too, if I have to. But I'm not going to be spoken to like that—and I'm not coming this afternoon.'

'My PA told me this morning that the press are waiting to talk to me. Elijah Vanaldi considering fatherhood is quite a story to them. I told her that I have nothing to say to them, but perhaps I should reconsider…' Still his hands held hers. 'They might be interested to hear that I have a fiancée—interested in her story too…'

'Why would they be interested in me?' Ainslie countered. 'You're the one who'll come across badly if you talk to the press. Ms Anderson will find out for sure…'

'She'll find out about our little ruse this afternoon if you don't come.' Elijah shrugged. 'So really there is nothing to lose…'

'For me either.' Ainslie shrugged, attempted nonchalance, but her heart-rate was quickening. The hands that held hers were not ready to let her go, and a mirthless smile twisted on his mouth as he delivered his threat.

'I'm a bit worried about your friend Angus though. He might not fare so well…'

'You wouldn't.'

'Just watch me!' He wasn't even pretending to smile now. 'I told you when you agreed to this that I would do whatever it takes, use whatever means I had available to protect my nephew. And if that means digging the dirt on some *celebrity* doctor I've never even met, then consider it done!'

* * *

Standing, clutching her drink, Ainslie eyed the eclectic gathering. Waitresses moved among the crowd, offering finger food and drinks to young mothers from Guido's playgroup, who didn't quite blend with the suits of the finance and property world. Other friends of Maria and Rico's reminisced with each other, whilst Rico's family stood huddled together, drinking copiously, throwing the occasional dark look to the only person who, despite Ainslie by his side, despite making polite talk and absolutely doing his duty, somehow stood utterly alone.

'Mr Vanaldi!' It was a less confrontational Ms Anderson who came over. 'About before.' She ran an eye around the room, at the strained subdued gathering, at the simmering grief and tension beneath the surface, and gave an apologetic nod. 'You were right not to bring Guido.'

'Thank you.' Graciously he accepted her admission. 'I was also at fault…I went too far…' Stilted though it was, his own apology was genuine, and Ainslie realised as his hand sought hers that it wasn't exclusively aimed at Ms Anderson—that in his own strange way he was apologising to her too. 'I know your intentions are good.'

'What are your plans for Christmas Day—for Guido?' Ms Anderson enquired.

'We will keep it quiet—but in the afternoon, once he has had his rest, your sister has offered to take Guido to my brother-in-law's relatives for a few hours. My driver will take them, and they can spend the afternoon and evening with him, then Enid will bring him back to his home.'

'That sounds good.' She gave a sympathetic smile, first to Elijah and then to Ainslie. 'You two really do seem to be doing well with him—under the most trying of circumstances.'

Not that well, Ainslie thought, seemingly the perfect fiancée, standing sombre and loyal by her partner's side—only this time it was Ainslie's hand not holding his in return.

This time it was Ainslie who, after the polite exchange with Ms Anderson, claimed back her hand and her personal space and slipped to the loo.

As was her privilege.

Over and over he stung her with his words.

Little barbs of poison injected to her heart that couldn't merely be soothed with an afterthought of an apology.

Barely recognising herself, she stared in the mirror. It wasn't just the elegant hair that was unfamiliar, or the perfectly applied make-up that made her look different. Neither was it the black angora dress that could never be considered *vulgar* that altered her reflection. No, it was the troubled eyes she didn't recognise. The turmoil in her soul that had her wretched. The attraction she felt for him, the tenderness he displayed when he held her, was so at odds with the torment he inflicted at times.

Well, no more. Running her hands under the tap, Ainslie collected her many thoughts before she headed back out there. She'd see it through today—see it through till after Christmas for Guido. But then she'd go. And if he did go to the press about Angus… A surge of panic welled inside, but she quashed it. A hundred thought processes whirred at once as she washed her hands, then reached into her bag to retouch her lipstick. Her mind still buzzing with anger, she hardly noticed the woman who came up behind her.

'*Molto conveniente.*' Ten days of solid brushing wouldn't

take away the yellow of the teeth that met her gaze as she looked over her shoulder in the mirror. The snarl of the lips made Ainslie stiffen as Dina Castella confronted her, safe in the knowledge that they were alone.

'I don't know what you mean.'

'This is very *conveniente*.' Dina's English wasn't as good as Elijah's, but she had no trouble getting her point across. 'Suddenly the rich playboy has *una bella* fiancée!'

'We just recently got engaged.'

'Come…' she sneered. 'Since when did Elijah Vanaldi make a commitment to a woman? Any woman! You think we wouldn't have heard about this in our village? You think I am stupid?'

'Of course not.'

'So how much?' Dina glared. 'How much does he pay you?'

'This has nothing to do with money!' Ainslie said through gritted teeth, but Dina just gave a mocking laugh and picked up Ainslie's shaking hand, eying her ring with distaste.

'You come very cheap.'

'It was their mother's ring…' Ainslie flared. 'As I said, this isn't about money.'

'Why would you lie for him, then?' Dina countered, her face twisting with suppressed rage. 'Because we both know that you are…' She must have seen Ainslie's flush of colour, or the constriction as her throat tightened, because she was quick to pounce. 'If it's money you need walk away now. We will be able to take care of you. Unlike the Vanaldis, with all their lies and stories, at least the Castellas, good or bad, tell the truth.'

CHAPTER NINE

LA VIGILIA DI NATALE.

Christmas Eve. Only it didn't feel like it.

During her time in London Ainslie had never really experienced homesickness, but she felt it now. She ached, just ached for a hot Australian summer, for blue skies and the sun burning on her shoulders as she dragged an overloaded trolley through a packed supermarket car park. And for *Carols By Candlelight* booming on the television as friends dropped over, sniffing the aromatic air as they stepped out onto the decking, where her father would guard the barbecue. For the familiar traditions that were *her* idea of Christmas instead of the hastily amalgamated traditions they must somehow pull together now if they were to give this little boy any semblance of the Christmas his parents would have wanted for him. Ainslie and Elijah had to weave together an English and Sicilian Christmas—to somehow fill this house with love and laughter and hopefully let some magic into Guido's life.

Even if only for a little while.

'In Sicily we eat fish on Christmas Eve: seven fish dishes…' He actually managed a smile at Enid's rather pained expression and added that one would do. 'Also—' his voice thickened '—children do not write to Santa. Instead they write to their parents, tell them how much they love them.'

'He's too young…' Enid attempted, but Elijah shook his head.

'Maria wrote for Guido last year—it was something she wanted to happen—something she did not really have herself. It should be placed under the father's plate, and he reads it at dinner. Maybe we should do it for Guido…' His eyes turned to Ainslie. 'Till he is old enough.'

Which made no sense.

Oh, the tradition made sense—just not the *we*, and not the implication that there was a future, that there would be more Christmases.

'That sounds lovely.'

Enid's voice snapped Ainslie back to bitter reality— even when mired in grief Elijah played to his audience, and she had to remember that. *Had* to stop blurring the reality, had to stop believing that the tender words he whispered, that the love he made to her when he came to her at night, was anything more to him than a pleasurable interlude in a hellish journey—an escape.

Her throat tightened as she recalled his cruel words… a perk!

'Are you okay, Ainslie?' Elijah frowned over.

'Just tired.' Ainslie gave him a tight smile that didn't meet her eyes. 'It's been a draining day.'

She hadn't told him about Dina—had chosen to leave that little gem for later. She first wanted to work out her own feelings on what Dina had said, wanted to try and work out her own truth before she added fuel to an already raging inferno and voiced her misgivings to him.

'Mummmm-mummm-mummm…' Guido hummed the words as they sat at the table, screwing up his little face at the food Enid attempted to shovel into his clamped mouth.

'It's good for you, Guido,' Enid soothed, taking the opportunity when Guido opened his mouth to protest to quickly get a loaded spoon in.

But Guido's manners hadn't improved, and even Ainslie's strained face broke into a smile as Guido almost perfectly re-enacted his performance on the underground, spitting out his food in disgust.

'He will learn manners in time, I suppose…' Elijah started, as Enid carried the angry bundle upstairs for a bath, but his shrewd eyes instantly took in Ainslie's pursed lips. 'What?'

'Nothing.' Ainslie's voice was tight. She was quashing down her anger as she fiddled with the stem of her wine glass. Tonight of all nights was surely not the one to row.

'Say what you are clearly thinking!'

'I'd rather not.'

'Please share…' Elijah goaded. 'Better out than in.'

'Not always!' A flash of tears in her eyes was rapidly blinked away. 'Maybe Guido *won't* grow out of it—maybe it's hereditary?'

'What?'

'Spitting in people's faces—hurting someone who doesn't deserve it.'

'Ainslie… I have already addressed that.'

'Actually, you haven't!' Her voice was rising and she struggled to smother it. 'You delivered an apology to Ms

Anderson which cryptically I was supposed to accept as aimed at me too. Well, no. You've signed me up for the gig, and whether I want to or not I guess I've got to play, but...'

Her voice trailed off as Enid returned, a clean and smiling Guido in her arms, dressed in powder-blue pyjamas, his dark hair a mass of curls and a gorgeous sleepiness in the those blue, blue eyes that were so much like Elijah's. Holding out his arms to Ainslie, coyly almost, he nestled his head in her arms when she held him, clinging to her like a barnacle on a rock as she sat at the table.

How could she walk?

Merely drop him and go?

Inhaling his baby smell, holding onto this little bundle that could be comforted and soothed by her mere presence, both terrified and comforted *her*. In just a few days her presence had settled Guido. It was her arms he often wanted when Enid brought him into the room, her that he toddled to as he ran giggling out of the bath. At some deep level this little guy, in a very short space of time, knew that he could trust her.

'Guido...' Elijah cleared his throat, pulled out a piece of paper. 'You are too young to write, but I know you feel—I know you do not understand, but I know you are confused...'

If she was his *real* fiancée she should be dabbing her cheek, or smiling bravely at him to continue, but because she wasn't Ainslie's nose ran into the little shoulder that was hooked into hers. Guido's thumb bobbed into his mouth. He was safe in his little world as the lady held him and the man spoke. Guido had no comprehension of the future that had been buried today, trusting as only a baby could that it was all going to be okay.

'Your *mamma* and *papà* loved you—how many times they told me that I cannot count—and they would be proud, would want to be with you now. I hope they are. All I promise tonight is that I will always be there for you.'

She could feel the delicious, heavy, weightlessness of sleep in Guido's body—could feel his mass of muscle relax as she held him. The ribbons of tension that bound him tightened for a second as Enid peeled him from her arms—and she could feel the awful heavy silence when it was only they two.

'You realise that I needed you there this afternoon.' It was Elijah who broke the silence. 'And that if you leave…well, I lose him.'

'Well, you got your way,' Ainslie said coolly. 'For now.'

'Ainslie, I am trying to do as you suggest—I am trying to trust these people, trying to believe that maybe they have changed. But I went over there today and they didn't so much as look at Guido, just asked if I had the money for them. Everyone is telling me to make peace, that I have got it wrong.'

'Got *what* wrong?' Ainslie frowned, then gave a shake of her head. His problems were his own now. 'Let's just try and get through tomorrow.'

'You must both be exhausted.' Enid said later, when she brought two mugs of hot chocolate through to the vast lounge.

Elijah rolled his eyes at the offering and poured himself a rather large brandy. 'Today has been made much easier by having you here,' he said, and Enid flushed with pleasure. 'We were lucky to get you at such short notice. It has made a huge difference.'

'It's made a huge difference to me too! Christmas isn't a time to be on your own.'

And Ainslie watched as Elijah dispensed with formality and poured Enid a brandy too, asking her to join them, even teasing her about the humongous turkey that had commandeered half the fridge.

'I make a lovely Christmas dinner—you wait till you taste my chestnut stuffing!' Enid said proudly. 'I'll serve it at midday—so there's plenty of time for Guido to have his nap before he goes to his aunt and uncle's.'

'You must join us.' Elijah frowned.

'I'll feed Guido.' Enid nodded. 'And make sure he behaves. But I won't intrude.'

'Please do!' Elijah said. 'And Tony too. Ainslie and I—' he took her hand and she bristled, she just couldn't play any more today, but Elijah hadn't finished with her yet '—will need all the help we can to make it a happy day for Guido.'

'The more the merrier?' Enid gave a sympathetic smile. 'Well, don't worry—we'll make it a special day for him. Even if we're not...' she faltered. 'I'm sorry, of course *you're* his family.'

'Not the one that was meant for him,' Ainslie said, taking her hand back and drinking her chocolate, preferring to talk about Enid's world than lie about her own. 'What about your own family?'

'There's just my sister,' Enid answered. 'But I don't want to always land on her doorstep. I worked for a lovely family for twenty-four years. I looked after the house and the children. The parents both travelled overseas a lot with their work.'

'They became your family?' Ainslie asked.

'We're still close—even when the youngest had left home they kept me on to mind the house—but they've moved to Singapore now. He got this job offer out of the blue, and the next thing I knew the house was for sale. Which leaves me—' she took a sip of her brandy '—well, a little bit lost, I suppose. That's why it's nice to be here. I'm going to look for a house to buy in the New Year.'

'I could help with that. It looks as if I'm going to be here for a while,' Elijah offered easily. 'If you want me to.'

'Oh, I don't think it would be anything close to the grand scale you're used to dealing with.'

'I know a lot of people,' Elijah said, 'and I know who not to deal with.'

'Oh, well, that would be wonderful. Thank you.' Enid looked as if a huge weight had been lifted off her shoulders as she stood up and said goodnight. 'Before I go to bed, do you want me to help setting up the presents?'

Ainslie was about to accept when annoyingly Elijah declined Enid's offer, and for the first time Ainslie got a real glimpse of being a parent.

They soldiered on long after exhaustion had hit, placing Maria's lovingly wrapped presents under the tree. Ainslie added her own hastily bought gifts, but even with the smell of pine in the air and the fairly lights left on, when Elijah turned off the main lights and the room was bathed in the tree's glow still it felt a world away from Christmas. For little Guido it was far too late to hope for a miracle.

'What are you doing?' Elijah asked as she crept into Guido's room.

'Tying a stocking to his cot!' Ainslie hissed, trying to do just that, and wincing as Guido stirred at the intrusion.

'You're waking him up!' Elijah whispered from the doorway.

'Done!' Ainslie joined him in the hall.

'He won't know any different…'

'Of course he'll know,' Ainslie assured him. 'It's Christmas—he'll know it's a special, magical day.'

'Not for him.' There was a break in his voice, another dent appearing in the armour he had clad himself in just to make it through the day, and he looked so ragged, so weary, so exhausted, it took everything she possessed not to raise her hand and capture his tired face, not to press her lips against his tense cheek, to be the one to lead him to bed, to lay him down and somehow kiss away his pain. Only tonight she just couldn't—his callous words still rang in her ears, and anger, hurt and humiliation were a strong antidote to need.

No, miracles were sadly lacking in this house. Especially when Elijah pushed open the bedroom door and Ainslie carried on walking.

'Where are you going?'

'To find another room…' She gave a small, tight smile. 'Thankfully there's an inexhaustible supply in this house.'

'Ainslie…' He followed her, stood at the door to the guest room—utterly gorgeous, still in the suit he had worn to the funeral, his tie in his pocket, as it had been when first they'd met. 'I am sorry for before. Please, it is Christmas Eve. My sister was—' His throat tightened on words he couldn't say. Only she had no reserves left, no well to dip the bucket in and come to the surface smiling. She just stood there drenched in bitterness as, instead of pleading his case, he spoke about practicalities. 'What about Enid? She will know we are sleeping apart.'

'Couples fight,' Ainslie said. She had never once used her body as a tease, and even by undressing in front of him she wasn't tonight. She was just tired to the marrow, and if he wasn't going to leave, then he could stand there and watch her sleep. Slipping off her black stockings and pulling on the soft white silk pyjama shorts that she'd chosen for herself, Ainslie wriggled out of her skirt as he stood there. But she *did* turn away as she unhooked her bra and slipped the top over her bosom before turning around to face him. 'Even *real* couples fight.'

'At Christmas?' Elijah attempted, but it didn't move her. She didn't want sex that was an apology—she wanted the real thing.

'Especially at Christmas,' Ainslie retorted, standing rigid.

'You're very good at telling people how it should be,' Elijah said. 'Very good at telling people how to get there— the trouble is you give them the compass and take the map.'

'What?'

'I needed you at the funeral today.'

'You ignored me.'

'That didn't mean I wasn't glad you were there.'

'What you said after—'

'Was wrong,' Elijah finished for her. 'Unforgivable, it would seem. I was angry—angry that I had listened to you, that I had believed maybe things could be different—and then, when I was proved right, I was angry again when you contradicted me in front of the social worker…' Their disappointment in each other simmered in the long silence. 'If I lose you, I lose Guido too.' He gave a tired shrug. 'It would seem I already have.'

He left her then—left her with just the scent of him and a final glimpse of his fatigued face.

Slipping into the cool bed and staring at the ceiling, Ainslie knew that if it was about winning a fight then seemingly she just had.

And if it was about making a point then Ainslie had done very well for herself.

But as she lay in an empty bed on Christmas Eve, twitching with insomnia, over and over his face whirred into her vision. Seeing the grooves of exhaustion, close-up witness to the agony he endured, she relived the dark day, *felt* the deep chasm of his grief, and knew, *knew* that she hadn't won a thing.

That tonight Elijah lay alone with his thoughts.

And that surely she'd let him down when he had needed her most.

CHAPTER TEN

HE KNEW!

Despite his tender age, despite the horrors of the previous days, somehow Guido knew today was special. For the first time he slept through the night. His eager squeals snapped Ainslie awake at six a.m., and as she headed to his room she collided with a very tousled Elijah, who stood in nothing more than a pair of black hipster trunks that left very little to the imagination. Ainslie flushed as she apologised to his naked chest. Actually, they left rather a *lot* to her imagination.

'*Buon Natale.*' His face bruised with lack of sleep, grumbling and surly, still Elijah set the tone and called a rapid truce, his mouth finding hers for a brief second, his hand pulling her in at the waist. 'Merry Christmas, Ainslie.'

The central heating must surely have been left on high overnight, Ainslie concluded, because this vast London house in the middle of an English winter was positively stifling. Her lips stung from his brief kiss, the taste of him lingering as Elijah scooped up Guido, who was holding the teddy she'd poked into his stocking, and carried him downstairs. Ainslie followed behind, smiling at the baby, but looking at his uncle's back. The keyboard of his ribcage had her jaw clenched. She wanted to reach out, to stroke the keys, wanted to play him like a piano. Wanted *not* to notice the luscious swell of his quads as he squatted down and chatted to Guido, wanted *not* to notice the heavenly flat planes of his abdomen as he stood up, or the swirl of hair around his mahogany nipples. But it was either that or look at his face—which was something she was having terrible trouble doing this morning.

'Everything okay?' Elijah frowned as she stared somewhere past his shoulder and nodded.

'Everything's fine,' Ainslie croaked, as Enid emerged from the kitchen, a pinny tied around her vast purple dressing gown and wearing a pair of reindeer ears and flashing Santa earrings. Ainslie could have kissed her for the effort she had gone to—so she did.

'Merry Christmas!' Enid beamed, not remotely fazed by Elijah's lack of attire as he came over and kissed her too.

'*Buon Natale!*' Elijah responded.

There was a smile fixed on Ainslie's face as Enid assumed the role of camera person, taking instructions from Elijah who had, in two seconds flat, worked out how his sister's digital camcorder operated. After a couple of goes Enid grasped it too, and she stood filming as Elijah headed over to the mountain of presents. Only somehow, as Elijah sat with his nephew, as he helped him open each gift in turn, Ainslie realised that her smile was there because it *was*. Watching Guido's delighted reaction, feeling the love and thought his mother had put into each and every loving gift, she was determined not to sit miserable—because this little slice of time Enid was capturing for Guido still had his parents' presence.

'Merry Christmas, Enid!' Elijah held out a parcel. 'You can stop filming now.'

'For me?'

Embarrassed, delighted, abashed, Enid opened her present—a vast box of luxury cosmetics, and on the top a silver envelope which she carefully opened.

'A spa retreat? My goodness!'

'A weekend away for you and a friend! To take at your leisure…' Elijah waved away her stammering thanks. '*We* thought you might need some time to unwind after putting up with us.' He shot Ainslie a look that emphasised the *we*.

'And just another little thing…' Ainslie said, retrieving Enid's gift and quickly tearing off the label that was signed from her alone, trying to remember that, for the housekeeper's benefit at least, they really were a couple.

Which meant she'd had to buy Elijah a gift, of course.

And somehow it had seemed important at the time that she didn't charge it to his credit card. It had been impossibly hard on her budget to buy for a billionaire who could have whatever his heart desired, and suddenly the stupid digital picture frame she'd bought for him seemed woefully inadequate as Elijah pulled it out of the gold wrapping paper. Biting on her bottom lip as he turned his present over, she saw an expression she couldn't read appear on his face for just a moment before he looked her in the eye.

'Thank you.'

And surely he was cross. Surely if she really was his fiancée, if she really *were* allowed to love him, she should have shown it better. This beautiful, expensive man should be pulling back meticulously giftwrapped scented paper, crowing in delight over Ferragamo wallets or Tiffany cuff-links, quirky little gifts that made him smile.

'There wasn't much time…' Inexplicably tears were pricking her eyes. 'What with Guido and everything…' Fleeing to the kitchen was easier than breaking down in front of them. Her lips clamped together as she tried to hold it in, sniffing back tears. She opened the fridge and stood, hoping the cool air would take the heat out of her face.

'Why did you rush off?'

'I'm just getting some milk for Guido.' She was still at the fridge, with her eyes screwed closed now, desperately trying to keep her voice sounding normal.

'Enid can get that!' Elijah pointed out. 'You didn't wait for your present.'

His hand was on her shoulder, turning her around to face him and her eyes blurred more as they came to rest on the box he was holding, the tears she'd been holding back spilling out when she opened it.

A ruby, surrounded by diamonds, dangled beautifully on a silver-coloured chain.

Silver-coloured because even to Ainslie's untrained eye this wasn't costume jewellery. No manufactured stone could ever be as deep and as blood-red and as mesmerising as this one, and only real diamonds could ever sparkle like these.

'It's too much…' She choked out the words, because it was too much. This was a gift befitting this man's *real* fiancée—not a quick fill-in. 'I should have spent more…' Her mind was darting, grabbing onto anything that flitted into it rather than facing the truth.

She *wanted* it to be real.

Wanted the hands that were now holding the pendant, the hands that were now going under her hair, the hands that had made love to her, to be hands she could hold…always.

'What are you talking about?'

'Your present…'

'I like it.' She wasn't sure if he was talking about her present or the jewel that, when he released the chain, slipped cool and heavy between her breasts. They both stared down, his hands still behind her hair, warm fingers on the back of her neck. Her nipples liked it too—popping out like two disloyal bookends each side of the ruby.

Disloyal because she didn't want him to know how much she wanted him.

But she did.

'It's too much,' Ainslie choked again. But Elijah was having none of it.

'You like nice things,' he teased. 'And we don't want you stealing.'

If it was a joke it wasn't funny. 'You know I didn't steal.'

'I did know—remember?'

He had known, and she did remember.

'Don't I get a kiss?'

'Why…?' Ainslie's voice was still laced with hurt. 'Isn't it just another perk of the job?'

Oh, God, why, instead of snapping back, did he have to smile at her anger? Why, instead of coming up with some crushing reply, did he kiss her angry face, kiss each salty tear and then her eyelashes?

'I say thoughtless things at times,' he whispered, absolutely echoing her thoughts. 'But then at other times…'

She didn't want to kiss him, but she did. As he traced her eyes, her cheeks, as his fingers traced her throat, she wanted him so badly on her mouth. Like eating hot porridge from the outside in, Ainslie thought faintly, as her mouth twitched with desire. Working through the warm bits when you really wanted the hot bit in the middle, with the thick golden honey on the top.

'No…' Her mouth said what her body couldn't.

'Why not?' He breathed the words into the shell of her ear, his tongue teasing the lobe. Both of his hands were behind her now, resting on the fridge, their lips their only contact, and for a crazy second she wanted to climb into the fridge behind her and cool her flaming body down. Either that or press it against him, grab his face in her hands and kiss him so hard he'd be sorry—sorry for teasing, sorry for playing, sorry for hurting her.

'We mustn't embarrass Enid!' It was an emergency response—albeit pathetic, Ainslie realized—but somehow appropriate as Enid herself came in, and Elijah broke contact with a lazy smile, his hands still pinning her.

'I don't get embarrassed!' Enid boomed.

But Ainslie did. Especially when Enid's eyes fell on the necklace and she put on her glasses to take a closer look. Elijah made a funny sucking noise as he chewed on his bottom lip, suppressing a smile as every eye in the room focussed on Ainslie's still rather flushed décolletage. Her wretched nipples were still standing to beastly attention as Enid took her time.

'Just lovely!' Enid announced. 'Certainly not fake!'

'Absolutely not,' Elijah agreed solemnly, then added, with a wink for Ainslie's benefit, 'You can always tell.'

Then there were the phone calls.

To her parents, her brothers, her sister. Ainslie felt awfully decadent, ringing Australia on the mobile phone he'd bought her—but, as Elijah had pointed out on several occasions, he'd rather she didn't use the home phone.

'You're all right, though, darling?' Ainslie could hear the knot of worry in her mother's voice.

'I'm fine,' Ainslie assured. 'I've got a really good job.'

'But you said that about the last one,' her mother pointed out. 'Look, if you need money, or things aren't working out, we'd want you to tell us.'

'And I would.' Ainslie lied. How could she not? They were in Australia, for goodness' sake—literally on the other side of the world. She was hardly going to ring them with every little drama. 'But there isn't anything to tell. Things just didn't work out with Angus and Gemma, and this other job came up at the perfect time.'

She gave a tiny grimace to Elijah, but he was on a call of his own, talking in Italian, his rich deep voice making it difficult for Ainslie to concentrate on what was being said. Just as she went to move to another room Elijah had the same idea, moving into the study and closing the door behind him.

'And they're nice?' her mother checked. 'This new couple you're working for?'

It was just so, so much easier not to correct her. Just so much easier to say yes.

Clearly Elijah had a fair amount of *Buon Natales* to get through, because he stayed in the study for ages. But somehow, *somehow*, it was still a magical Christmas— somehow a little miracle did occur. Because despite the grief and despair of before, everyone did their best to make it happy. Everyone in the house gave everything they could to make it a special Christmas for a very special little boy.

Elijah, when he finally emerged from his calls, was loose and funny for once, stubbornly refusing to get dressed till long after breakfast, which consisted of strong coffee and thick wedges of *panettone* that melted on Ainslie's tongue as she bit into the candied orange and lemon zest. Christmas carols sang out from the television as Enid set to preparing Christmas dinner, and Elijah played with his new toy, taking out the memory stick from his sister's camera and placing it into the digital frame. Guido was delighted as images of himself and his parents whirred again and again before his eyes.

'Homesick?' Elijah caught her in a pensive moment as she stared out over her wine glass.

Coming down from the bedroom, showered and scented with Enid's gift of bath oils, and dressed up for Christmas dinner, she had caught her breath as she'd seen the table Enid had laid. The huge dining room had shrunk somehow with love. Holly and crackers and candles and vast bowls of satsumas decorated and scented the table, and a turkey that would surely feed them till *next* Christmas proudly took centre stage. It had hit her then—hit her as she'd sat down and seen Elijah, all clean and shaved and dressed up for dinner too, in an immaculate fitted white shirt over dress trousers, not smiling a brave smile, but actually managing to have fun. And when Tony had joined them, and they'd pulled crackers, and this great brute of a man had sat with a party hat on as they had all laughed at silly jokes, and Guido's smiling face had been replaced with utter disgust as he'd spat out his Brussels sprouts. It had hit her that somehow they'd made it work. This hastily arranged patchwork job of a family had somehow got it right—had somehow managed to find Christmas.

'Yes.' She answered his question honestly—because she *was* homesick.

Not at this moment for Australia, though, and not at this moment for her family.

Instead she was homesick for the future—for the nostalgia that would surely hit her whenever she looked back and remembered this day.

'We'll be back about seven, then!' Enid buttoned up Guido's coat as Tony took the nappy bag and stroller to the car. 'In time for Guido's bedtime.'

'Thank you for this!' Elijah thanked her, then bent to kiss his nephew. 'Be good for Enid,' he warned.

'He won't be!' Ainslie giggled as the door closed.

'I didn't want her here,' Elijah admitted, 'but she's actually been wonderful.'

'She has,' Ainslie agreed, suddenly shy and awkward now that they were alone, and wondering what to say next. Only she didn't have to—it was Elijah who broke the rather awkward silence as they sat down by the fire.

'I'm sorry.' And it wasn't thinly veiled, or aimed in her general direction, it was absolutely directed at her, and he stared right into her eyes. For the first time since the funeral, since his horrible, horrible words, they were properly alone. 'I was bitter and sad, angry and…' He struggled for a moment to find the word. *'Confuso?'* he offered.

'Confused?' Ainslie suggested.

'It is not a word I normally use…' He pushed out a breath. 'Normally I know exactly what to do—what I am doing, what needs to be done. Confused is not me. I took it out on you—and for that I am sorry.'

'You'll work it out,' Ainslie said. 'You're doing so well with Guido and…'

'It is not just Guido I am confused about.'

Sapphire eyes held hers.

'Then what?'

'Us.' He said it so simply it was Ainslie who was confused now. 'This was not what I was expecting.'

Which made sense—it was the only thing in this crazy life they had created that did make sense. Except for his kiss.

A kiss that had been needed last night, a kiss that had been waiting in the wings the whole morning. When finally their lips met she sobbed with longing, trembled at the feel of his mouth as it came home to hers. A kiss that made sense because to deny it would be illogical. To not move her mouth with his, to not capture his tongue as it parted her lips would be denial to the nth degree.

White cashmere stroked her face as he slid her jumper over her head and the cool of late afternoon greeted her flesh—despite the heating, despite the fire. But she only felt it for a trice. Elijah, kneeling on the floor now, pulled her into the warm embrace of his arms as he kissed her again. His expert hands dealt with her bra and his expert lips moved where his eyes had been since before breakfast. His black hair stroked her chest as his mouth worked on, his hand fiddling with the zipper of her skirt, still suckling as he guided her bottom, making light work of her skirt and panties till she was naked except for her shoes.

'Elijah!' Embarrassed to be so very naked whilst he was still so very dressed, she moved to right the imbalance. Only he wasn't listening, was pushing her back on the sofa in one easy motion and pulling her bottom down in a seemingly practised manoeuvre.

'Relax,' Elijah growled—and she promptly didn't! Between intimate kisses he ripped off his jumper and set back to work. 'Relax,' he said again, diving eagerly between her legs.

'I can't...' she quivered, wondering if she should just fake it to get it over with. She was assailed with visions of Enid walking in, banging her gloves before releasing Guido from his stroller, but—oh, heavens above—it did feel nice.

'I put the chain on the door.' He countered her thoughts, countered her everything. With every wriggle of her discomfort his concentration deepened—as if he was actually enjoying himself.

'I *want* to do this...' He answered her thought and suddenly she didn't want to think, couldn't really think of anything other than this. Couldn't think of anything other than Elijah, with his soft, soft lips, coaxing her with little flicks of his masterful tongue, sucking her most tender centre as she swelled beneath him. A moan began building in her throat, her fingers knotting in his hair now, and he read each gasp, each guttural moan, just did it so right she was putty in his hands. She could see her knees trembling, could see her thighs convulsing, could feel his hot breath, the dart of his tongue. And then he stopped, for a beat of a second that had her weeping. 'It is *my* privilege.'

He captured her clandestine pulse with his lips till there was surely nothing else to give, nothing else to take. He depleted every reserve till she was utterly spent, and only then did he kneel up, looking into her reeling eyes as he pulled her down in front of the fire. She could see him rising over her, see the curved outline of his shoulder in the fading light, hear the last spits of the fire as it died, unattended, and glimpsed the potent length of his erection that replenished her. She felt the greedy relish of an inexhaustible supply as he stabbed inside, her name a mantra as he said it over and over, as he bucked inside, as he sent her into freefall.

'I feel guilty for feeling…' He didn't finish his sentence. He didn't have to. The fire had gone out, the light had long since gone. Just the fairy lights guided them.

'I know.'

'With all that has happened.' He was on his back, his chest rising with each breath, his stomach hollow as her fingers played with his dark mass of hair. 'You change my life.'

Her hand stilled as she heard the reverence in his words. The dewy glow of their lovemaking was too long gone for these utterances.

'You've changed mine too…'

His curse wasn't perhaps the expected response, but was entirely merited when the door was buckling under the weight of its chain—and a frantic thirty seconds ensued. They pulled on clothes and hid knickers, arriving breathless and drunk on guilt to open the door as Enid marched in, with Tony carrying a dozing Guido, and promptly stamped her feet and banged her gloves.

'You're sure about letting me use Tony to take me to my sister's?'

'Absolutely,' Elijah unusually enthused—just a hint of colour on his normally deadpan face. 'How was it?'

'Okay.' Enid shrugged, breathing white air in the hallway as winter followed her in, picking up a bag of presents for her family. 'What did you two do?'

'Oh…' A useless liar at the best of times, Ainslie turned puce. 'This and that. So, how were the Castellas?'

'Much the same.' Enid gazed sadly over to Guido 'They didn't go to much effort. Still, they bought him a lovely present…all little glove puppets of animals. They got it at the airport in Italy for him. It's here…' She started rummaging beneath the stroller, but Elijah halted her.

'You've done enough—go to your sister's now, and have time with your family.'

'It's no trouble for me to put the little one to bed.'

'No,' Elijah insisted. 'We can manage.'

'Well, if you're sure,' Enid said, turning for the door and then changing her mind. 'I can't say I was expecting to, but I've actually had a really lovely day—it's been a wonderful Christmas. Oh, and Mr Vanaldi, just so you know—' this time as she headed for the door she didn't turn around '—you've got your jumper on inside out.'

Ainslie adored that he blushed.

Even a few hours later, as they lay in bed, he simultaneously stroked her thigh and gnashed his teeth in a wince when Ainslie suddenly remembered how they'd been caught. His sallow cheeks actually darkened as over and over she tried another tack to dispute what Enid must have thought.

'Maybe we were trying on our new Christmas presents?'

'Ainslie…'

'Or we got too hot…' She let out a peal of nervous laughter, then a groan. 'She thinks I'm a nymphomaniac— I mean, she's always catching us. She even told me off for leaving my wet nightdress at the bottom of the shower.'

'She'll think we're acting like any normal engaged couple,' Elijah soothed, and changed the subject. 'Actually, my friend Roberto would dispute that—but then his fiancée isn't anywhere near as good-looking as you.'

'And we don't have the ghastly pressure of a wedding to put us off!' Ainslie attempted, but it was hopeless, and they both knew it—especially with what he offered next.

'Maybe we just found each other?'

And she wanted him to seal it with a kiss, wanted him to take her in his arms and kiss her again. But Elijah was suddenly pensive.

'They stopped to buy a present?' Elijah frowned. 'When I heard the news I took my passport, wallet and laptop. I had to buy a phone charger and adapter plug at the airport…it wouldn't have entered my head to buy Guido a present.'

'People react differently, I guess,' Ainslie said, and though she didn't want to spoil the moment, somehow she knew honesty must prevail. 'Dina said something to me at the funeral.' He didn't push, didn't say anything—just held her till she was ready to reveal. 'She didn't say it directly, but—well, she offered me money to leave you…' And she waited for the rip to drag her under, for the inevitable explosion, only it never came—two strong arms wrapped more tightly around her.

'Sleep now.' Elijah kissed her hair. 'It's okay.'

He could feel her relax in his arms—her problem shared,

perhaps, but not halved. He was tempted to rouse her from her slumber, to tell her his fears. But what purpose could that serve? And if he did tell her—why would she stay?

Staring down, he saw the cupid's bow of her mouth, her eyelids flickering in sleep that eluded him, and he *wanted* her to leave—wanted to wake her now and tell her to get out of the cesspit he was exposing her to.

Guido.

His brain tightened, his heart pounding in his chest as it struggled to keep rhythm with the sudden division of loyalties—wanting her to go, needing her to stay.

Needing *her*.

'Go to sleep.' He said it out loud again, only this time to Maria—to the soul he could feel hovering, guarding her baby, willing him to listen. 'I will take care of it—*Buon Natale*.'

CHAPTER ELEVEN

'HE SHOULD be with Enid.'

'Sorry?' Creeping back into bed at dawn, having settled Guido, Ainslie frowned into the darkness.

'Enid should be the one getting up to him at night. She is employed as a live-in housekeeper and nanny—it should not be you getting up to him.'

'I don't mind, though…' Ainslie yawned, hoping to get back to sleep, waiting for the warmth of his arms. But whatever they had found last night seemed to be fading with the dawn.

'It is not a question of minding—if you were my real fiancée you would not be waking to a baby all night—I will have his crib moved in the morning,' Elijah said, his mind made up, and rolled on his side, away from Ainslie.

But she was having none of it. She sat up in bed and talked to his broad shoulders, watching them stiffen as she defied his sudden decisions.

'If I were your real fiancée I certainly *would* be waking up to him—and if I were your *real* fiancée, then we'd be discussing this sort of thing, rather than you jackbooting about, giving out orders.'

'Then it's just as well that you're not.'

Watching Tony take down the crib and move it up to the top floor, Ainslie felt as if she herself were being dismantled—everything she sometimes glimpsed in Elijah, the man she so foolishly had thought she was getting to know, had been taken and moved and put back together again. Only no matter how she looked, how she tried to pretend it was okay, it didn't fit its new surrounds.

'I'm going out for the afternoon.' Elijah found her in the master bedroom, standing where Guido's crib had been, staring out of the window and glimpsing Guido's future.

'Is that how it's going to be for him?' Ainslie turned to face him. 'Left to be amused by the nanny while you go out? Sleeping out of earshot so he doesn't disturb your rest?'

'You blow things out of proportion.'

'No, Elijah, I don't. What the hell could be so important that you have to go out on Boxing Day? Ms Anderson's right—this should be time you're spending with him, forging some sort of bond, not distancing yourself…distancing him.'

'Guido doesn't seem to mind—he's downstairs with Enid, playing with his new things.'

'He's fifteen months old, for goodness' sake!'

'Exactly my point!' Elijah shrugged, but didn't leave it there. 'In fact, the only person who seems to have a problem with my going out is you, which leads me to question your motives, Ainslie. Don't use my nephew to try and trap me with a guilt trip, just to satisfy your own curiosity. I'm going out.'

And in that lull between Christmas and New Year, when

you never knew if the post office or the bank was open, when the decorations were still up and there was no need to go out because the fridge was full to bursting, it was almost as if the universe gave people a chance to find each other. Only Elijah didn't seem to want to take it.

Elijah paced the floors as if he were in some tiny enclosure. When he wasn't on the phone, or in the study on his computer, he ignored the services of his driver and took himself out at every opportunity, leaving Ainslie to amuse herself and giving herself plenty of time to think.

'I'll be a couple of hours.'

'You're going to work?' Enid blinked, voicing Ainslie's thoughts exactly. 'Why?'

'There are a couple of properties I want to look at.'

As Enid shrugged and headed out of the kitchen Elijah explained further. 'I have a lot of properties in London—a lot of contacts. There's no reason to stop working just because I'm stuck here.'

'*Stuck* here?'

'I didn't mean it like that.'

'But it's the holidays.'

'Which means bills are starting to come in—the perfect time to put in a low offer.'

'And make a fortune out of other people's misery?'

'It's my job.' Elijah shrugged. 'And one I do well. Buy yourself something for the New Year's party—it will be black tie, which means—'

'I know what black tie means!' Ainslie snapped.

'I was about to say that we'll have to ask Enid to babysit. Can you see to that?'

'I'll tell Tony too.'

'We're getting a lift with friends—I've given Tony the night off.'

Oh, it was a very nice life—if that was what you wanted.

A babysitter on hand and a driver to whisk her wherever she wanted to go. Trailing around the shops whilst Tony walked behind her, carrying the bags. Her mission was to choose a new wardrobe for little Guido more befitting his new status, and, on Elijah's instructions, a set of luggage for him too, in readiness for his upcoming jet set existence. Oh, and an outfit for herself for the New Year's Eve party Elijah had told her they were going to.

Told her.

A very nice life for some. Only it wasn't what Ainslie wanted—not for her and certainly not for Guido.

Especially when that night *again* Elijah missed Guido's bath and bedtime. When *again* his 'couple of hours' stretched to midnight, and dinner out was apparently required to close whatever deal was being made. When he climbed in bed beside her, even though he pulled her in close, Ainslie could sense his distraction, could feel the restless energy beside her. She knew he was working up to telling her something, staring at the curtains before finally he managed to say what was on his mind.

'I might have to go to Italy for a few days…'

'You can't take Guido out of the country.'

'I know…' Elijah gave a long sigh. 'We have to go to this party on New Year's Eve, but then I have to go. I'll fly out on New Year's Day.'

'But surely…' Ainslie bit her tongue. She didn't want to

nag, didn't want to question, but shivers of jealousy and doubt seemed to be climbing up her oesophagus. That he could even *think* of leaving now was an enigma to her. 'You've got an appointment with Ms Anderson on the second.'

'Which you're going to have to handle. Look, Ms Anderson has to realise that I have a life, a job—a job that I've put on hold since the accident. I have commitments, employees. I walked out on my life with two minutes' notice—surely, *surely*,' he hissed, 'she should be able to accept that I have things to do.'

How did he do it? Ainslie wondered. How did he make the unreasonable so reasonable? How did he always manage to twist things till the impossible made perfect sense?

Well, not this time.

'He's your *nephew*, Elijah.' She turned to face him. 'Your orphaned nephew who you're engaged in a bitter custody battle to keep. The Castellas are ringing every day—you know as well as I do that the second you leave the country they're going to demand he stay with them.'

'He will stay here!' Elijah retorted. 'In his home. And you are to be with him at all times—if the Castellas come to the door they are not to be let in. Look, if you're not up to dealing with the appointment I will ring Ms Anderson to reschedule, but the fact is I have things to attend to, and if that deems me an unsuitable surrogate father—then maybe I am.'

'You have no intention of changing, do you?'

'Why should I?' Elijah retaliated. 'Unlike you—I actually *liked* my old life. Off to the spare room again?' he drawled, as Ainslie sprang out of bed and pulled on her wrap. 'Are you going to run off every time you don't get your own way?'

'I was going to the loo, actually,' Ainslie bit back, heading down the hall and sitting on the edge of the bath, dragging in air and trying to calm down. But she couldn't.

Every word he'd said made seemingly perfect sense.

Only to Ainslie it didn't.

She could sense the shift that had occurred, could almost feel him slipping away…and not just from her, from little Guido too.

'You *should* go out.' Enid was utterly insistent.

Feeling guilty as all hell, Ainslie ducked her face from Guido's wet kisses so as not to spoil her professionally applied make-up. Wrapped in a bathrobe, so as not to blemish her rapid tan, and a silk scarf to keep her false curls from frizzing, Ainslie fed Guido his turkey and mash.

'It's New Year's Eve,' Enid pushed on. 'And if you are going to have Guido—well, he's going to have to get used to the fact you two go out.'

'But we won't as much.' Ainslie shivered, trying to say the right thing, but finding it harder with each and every word.

Elijah's mobile phone was constantly trilling, and his laptop was always on. Invitations thudded onto the mat as the world caught up to the fact that Elijah Vanaldi was in town. The thought of spreading her wings and fluttering into Elijah's real world had her dripping in cold sweat, but all that she could deal with—all that she could cope with blindfolded—if Elijah just met her halfway. If the man she had glimpsed, the uncle Guido so richly deserved, might somehow return.

Dragging her mind back to the conversation, Ainslie

knew she was trying to convince herself as much as Enid. 'We won't be going out as much. Not now we've got Guido to think of.'

'Of course you will,' Enid huffed in her no-nonsense way. 'I Googled him.'

'Googled him?'

'Mr Vanaldi—Elijah. So don't try and tell me that you two don't love the high life—your life isn't going to suddenly stop, so off you go and enjoy yourselves. After all you've been through you both deserve it.'

Maybe they did.

Maybe a night out *was* just what they needed. Perhaps she was starting to go stir-crazy, confined to the house and the park. Elijah was used to parties and glamour and running on adrenaline. Of course it couldn't just end because of Guido—he'd work out a compromise, and tonight so would she!

Staring in the full-length mirror, Ainslie almost had herself convinced! The pale pink raw silk, hand-beaded dress with matching coat had looked appalling on the hanger—like some rosé impersonation of the Christmas tree in the lounge. But once on—once set against a backdrop of spiralling blonde curls and a necklace to die for, with indecently high soft grey stilettos and lashings of silver eyeshadow—somehow, *somehow* it worked.

Unlike them.

Everything they'd found at Christmas seemed lost. The hands that had adored her hadn't been near her in days, the mouth that had kissed her derisive now, and she truly didn't get him—couldn't fathom that he would consider leaving for Italy so close to Social Services making its decision.

That he should simply walk away from something he insisted he wanted.

'You look lovely!' Enid beamed as Ainslie tripped down the stairs. 'Tony's in the kitchen—I'm just making him a cuppa.'

While we wait for Elijah.

She didn't say it, of course. It wasn't really the housekeeper's place to point out that Prince Charming was late for the ball.

Ainslie was so distracted she forgot Elijah's instructions not to answer the phone. She picked it up unthinking on the second ring, to find there in her hand and in her ear Elijah's real world: a throaty, sexy voice, talking in rapid Italian, purring like a kitten as Ainslie attempted to find her own voice.

'Elijah isn't here.'

'And you arrrre?'

She dragged her rrr's, Ainslie noted. The kitten showing its claws?

'Ainslie.'

'Oh—the stand-in!' A peal of laughter pierced her eardrum. 'Don't worry, Elijah told me about the old housekeeper, and that I must be careful.'

Something died a little inside Ainslie as Enid came out and placed a mug on the hall table.

'I can be discreet when I have to. Where is he? His mobile is off.'

'Who are you?' It was the bravest, yet possibly the most stupid of questions—one she'd already envisaged the answer to, even before it came.

'It's Portia!' came the confident reply—as if she should

already know, as if she really shouldn't have been so stupid as to think that a guy like Elijah came with his wings already clipped. 'His *real* girlfriend.'

After arriving home with about two minutes to spare, not even bothering to apologise, Elijah had washed and changed in a matter of moments, cursing as he did up his tie and combed back his hair. Dousing himself in cologne, he neither commented on her looks nor her mood.

But he noticed.

Could see her taut and pale in the mirror, more beautiful and fragile than he had ever seen her.

He didn't want to ask how she was, because it would kill him to hear.

Didn't want another row. Didn't want to justify going out when he didn't want to either.

He hated that he was going tomorrow.

Hated that he was making her stay.

Only he didn't want her to leave either.

'Come!' He offered his hand, knowing she wouldn't take it. 'Let's go.'

Elijah's *friends* were as awful as her mood. She hardly caught their names, and then they were chatting loudly and rudely in Italian as the driver whizzed them the couple of miles to their destination—a luxury residence with glittering views of the river, champagne flowing and a discreet procession of waiters bringing around the most delectable of finger food. But no amount of champagne could console her, and food, no matter how delectable, couldn't give her comfort tonight.

Elijah had introduced her to a small group, given her a

glass and then disappeared, as if dropping a dog off at the kennels, leaving her standing amongst his yapping social set, who were a different breed entirely. She tried to fit in, tried to blend and make small talk, but she was out of kilter—not just a step behind this glamorous, jet setting crowd, but lapped again and again. She listened without interest to talk of skiing holidays and nannies who had the nerve to want the night off on New Year's Eve!

And they all adored Elijah.

Ainslie had to grit her teeth as she attempted conversation, while out of the corner of her eye she watched as female after female came to offer him their condolences. Rather like the line-up Elijah had declined to take part in at the funeral. He consented now, accepting their kisses. Some were moved to tears—though not enough to mess up their make-up, Ainslie noted bitterly. But, hell, she *felt* bitter.

Bitter with him, bitter that these people, these awful, obnoxious people, could mean so much to him—that the man who measured up in so many departments failed so miserably in the one that mattered most.

'Come.' As the hands of the clock crept towards midnight he graced her with a dance, but it was way too little and way too late. He'd ignored her all night, too busy chatting up his rich banking friends to even *bother* chatting up her. She had tried not to be jealous, tried to remember she was here for Guido's sake. She'd tried to remember it wasn't his job to care about her. But after she'd seen him so relaxed and carefree in the expensive surroundings, seen the glitter of want in other women's eyes, her self-loathing was toxic—because, despite herself, despite everything, still she wanted him to.

Wanted him in way she had never wanted another.

Wanted not just a piece of him, but exclusive rights—something she was sure he was incapable of giving.

She knew that soon he'd tire of her—just as he had with Guido.

His hands were loose around her waist as they swayed, and it appalled her how much she wanted to rest in his arms, on his chest, to hold him, to smell him, to feel him just one more time. But she fought it, held back when she wanted to give in, ignored each pleading beat of her heart and resisted the call of her body.

'At least try to *pretend* you're enjoying yourself,' he hissed in her ear.

'Why?'

'Why?' His single word was shot with incredulity and frustration.

'These people are awful—I've tried talking to them—and you've ignored me all night…'

'Ainslie,' Elijah interrupted, 'you've got all the symptoms of postnatal depression without actually having given birth. And I've told you—I have to talk to these people.'

'To Portia too?'

His hand twisted on her elbow, guided her out to the freezing balcony, and his palpable anger was enough to have the remaining smoker take his last gasp before midnight then stub it out and run in.

'She rang tonight.'

'I have told you not to answer the phone.' Elijah shrugged. 'It's hardly my fault if you choose to ignore my instructions. Thank you for passing on the message.'

'I haven't yet.' Her voice twisted with bitterness. 'She

said she's your *real* girlfriend—that's what she told me. I guess it's your job to convince me otherwise.'

'Do you really think I didn't have a life before this happened?'

'Is she the reason you're going to Italy?'

'Portia?' He had the audacity to laugh. 'You think I am going for *Portia*?'

'Is that who you've been on the phone to all week?'

'You're jealous?'

'Yes!' Ainslie roared. 'And I'm sorry if I'm not worldly enough or sophisticated enough to say it doesn't matter that you're sleeping with her as well as me. But tell me this, Elijah, would your *real* girlfriend get up to your nephew at night? Would your *real* girlfriend love Guido the way I do? Would your *real* girlfriend—?' She stopped herself there—stopped because she didn't dare tell him she loved him, couldn't give him any more ammunition to fling at her when she was spent already.

'I never got round to finishing things with her.'

She winced at his disregard, knew that when her time came she'd be treated just as brutally.

'You are so ready to think the worst of me.' Elijah shook his head at her reaction. 'Between the hospital and the undertaker and the lawyers and the funeral I forgot to tell the woman I had been seeing for all of two weeks that there was no place in my life for her. Ainslie, believe me when I say I have not given Portia a thought. I rang her yesterday and told her what had happened. But I was giving her an excuse, not a reason—and I was also trying to find out some information. You are right—Portia could never come close to all you have given…'

She could feel his breath on her cheeks, see the anger, the passion in his eyes that matched hers.

'In this hell I never expected to be happy. I feel guilty that I can smile, that you make me laugh, that I can hold you and forget when my mind should be on Guido, on my sister. That with all that is happening every hour I want you!'

And then he kissed her—kissed her because he couldn't make her leave, kissed her because, no matter how much he wanted her gone, still he wanted her here. His mouth claimed hers, because it was his, but she fought it, tightened her lips. His tongue probed and, like a hot knife through butter, they parted. He tasted of champagne and he smelt of reckless danger. Hot, hard kisses didn't belong in this argument, this passion that blurred the lines over and over, this want that made her weak.

She could hear the chant of the crowd, counting down to the New Year, and all it did was terrify her. She wanted him one last time before she gave up the addiction that was Elijah. She didn't want twelve o'clock to strike, didn't want it to be tomorrow—because then she'd have to give him up.

His hands weren't loose on her waist, as they had been on the dance floor, they were pulling her right into him. His mouth was pressing on hers and she was kissing him, loving him and hating him all at the same time as every chime of Big Ben rang in the New Year. This celebration was nothing in Australia, but it was massive here. Everyone, from the party inside, to the people on the balconies below and in the street beneath, was breaking into 'Auld Lang Syne', and still he kissed her, his erection pressing into her as he pushed her into the wall behind. He could have taken her there, and the fact that she wanted him to take her, that with every twist of the kaleidoscope somehow she always wanted him, made her loathe him all the more.

'I hate how you make me.' She was crying the more he kissed her, but still she kissed him back.

'You love how I make you.' His mouth consumed hers, his tongue lashing hers, flailing her with every stroke.

He kissed the breath out of her all the way in the taxi back home, kissed her up the steps and through the front door, kissed her all the way into the hall and up the stairs.

She'd give up first thing, Ainslie promised herself as her fingers coiled in his hair, as she kissed him back with a frenzy that matched his, as they made it to the bedroom but not to the bed.

He was pushing up her dress as he sucked at her neck, unleashing his fierce erection and then tearing at her knickers. Rough fingers were parting her thighs, and even though she was in killer heels he had to lower himself to enter her. It was uncomfortable as he stabbed inside her, but somehow it was tender. This raw need that consumed them both would soon would be soothed with sweet release. His palms pressed into her hips, his fingers digging into her bottom, holding her, supporting her as he warmed her core. With each thrust he satisfied her yet had her wanting more—more of him. Her orgasm dragged him in deeper, and she was clinging on tighter with each intimate beat as he pulsed inside her, a heady rush consuming her as he groaned out her name.

When it was over—when later they were lying in bed, waiting for the morning that would take him away—he said the words she'd dreaded.

'Marry me…'

Under any other circumstances it wouldn't have hurt to hear him ask—only this wasn't about love, and it wasn't uttered in a moment's liberation post-orgasm. Ainslie knew that. This was about Elijah moving his pawns into place, Elijah thinking ahead, Elijah working the board to claim what he considered his. Two little words she had somehow known were coming from a man who knew how weak she was for him. She was terrified that she'd say yes, wondered how she could possibly find the strength to say no.

'Don't answer yet.' He hushed her troubled mind with his lips. 'We'll talk when I return.'

And, because she was at his bidding, Ainslie didn't know whether that gave her a few hours or maybe a few days to come up with her answer.

CHAPTER TWELVE

ELIJAH'S impeccable work ethic didn't quite translate to his home life. There was no call to check on Guido, and he certainly didn't ring to check on Ainslie. And wherever he'd left the message for Ms Anderson it hadn't been delivered!

'This really is most irregular.' Less than impressed, Ms Anderson had checked on a sleeping Guido and was now grilling Ainslie in the formal lounge.

'He has to work,' Ainslie defended. 'He has things that need to be sorted. He left everything when the accident happened, so he's taking a couple of days to clear things up so that he can come back and concentrate on Guido.'

'Which will be when?' Ms Anderson pushed. 'I want to see him with his nephew—see how they're interacting.'

'Elijah should be back in a couple of days,' Ainslie said firmly,

'Well, make sure that he is! The Castellas are going to be most upset, and frankly I don't blame them. If he can't be with his uncle, surely he should be with the rest of his family.'

'Guido's at home here…' Ainslie swallowed, trying desperately to remain assertive. 'To move him now, for a couple of days while Elijah is away, would just unsettle him.'

'I know that,' Ms Anderson snapped. 'I hope your fiancé realises that if it wasn't for you, if it wasn't for the fact you're his fiancée and are presumably going to have a large part in Guido's life, I'd have no hesitation in allowing Guido to spend some time with his other relatives—and I'll be telling the Castellas that. You can tell Mr Vanaldi too. His money doesn't impress me—I do not want this little boy raised by a string of hired help when there's a loving family who dearly want him.'

Keeping in her sigh of relief when Ms Anderson picked up her bag and made to leave, Ainslie saw her to the door. 'I'll have him ring you as soon as he returns.'

'See that he does!'

'Her bark's worse than her bite!' Teatowel in hand, Enid found Ainslie letting out her breath against the closed door.

'Is it?' Never had she been more grateful for Enid's solid presence. Bone-tired from it all, Ainslie let herself be taken to the kitchen. She sat in the womb-like refuge Enid offered and sipped on tea and dunked biscuits. Like fighter pilots scrambling, her brain tried to locate its target.

Only it kept moving.

'Maybe she's right,' Ainslie said finally, and Enid stopped unloading the dishwasher and came and sat down. 'I mean, if Elijah can miss such an important appointment because of work what else is he going to miss? The Christmas play? Parent-teacher interviews? Bathtime?'

'He's got things to sort out…' Enid soothed, but Ainslie shook her head.

She'd Googled him too—and any doubt she'd had that Portia might be the reason Elijah had gone to Italy had been quashed. Elijah, it would seem, didn't even stretch to dinner and a hand-hold to dump a girlfriend—from the bitter interviews she'd read, several women would have considered themselves lucky if they'd even got a text message. Which left work the only reason he was there. And that didn't fare any better with Ainslie, because if commitments *had* to come first, then where did that leave Guido?

And where did it leave her?

A convenient wife?

She could almost glimpse it, and it terrified her.

She was terrified that she'd accept his diamond crumbs, accept his lifestyle, accept his lovemaking, accept all he would offer, if it meant he would come home to her—while all the time knowing that if circumstances had been different he'd never have given her a second glance.

'I don't know what to do.' Helpless, Ainslie turned to Enid, sought guidance even though she couldn't reveal the whole truth. 'I don't know what is best for Guido—maybe he *would* be better with the Castellas. Just because Elijah loves him, it doesn't necessarily mean he's right.'

'Are you getting cold feet, pet?' Enid poured more tea. 'I can't say I blame you—with the life your fiancé leads it's going to be you raising him. And before you ask I'm not going to say anything to my sister. She's good enough at her job,' Enid said, not just loyally but with honesty. 'She really will do her best to work out what's best for Guido.'

'The perfect nuclear family, you mean?'

'No,' Enid said.

'Does she even *have* kids?' Ainslie's voice was rising now, but Enid stayed calm.

'Her girlfriend does…' Enid gave a small smile at Ainslie's raised eyebrows. 'So she more than most knows it isn't necessarily about a mum and a dad, nor a father who makes it home each night—it's about a loving household. Which this is.'

Oh, it was—for Ainslie at least. The fighter pilots had located their target now and were taking aim at her very core.

She loved him.

Which blurred everything.

Love, as Ainslie was fast realising, was a crazy thing, that made you rewrite your rules, that made a mockery of your own questions, that told you to just keep quiet when maybe you should speak up.

And speak up she would!

She would demand the truth before she made her decision—not just about where he had been, but about where they were going. To live without his love would be agony enough, but to live by his rules would be hell.

Her own rules were simple, Ainslie realised—honesty and respect were a small price for him to pay if she gave him her heart.

A touch calmer after her decision, if not entirely happy, for the first time since they'd met she let the world in. She decided she'd ring a couple of her old nanny friends this evening and see if they were interested in catching up some time. Picking up the paper for the first time in the longest time, she actually read—caught up with events instead of just reading her horoscope—and smiled at the sound of Guido waking over the intercom.

'I'll go,' Enid said.

'No, I will…' She went to stand, but froze midway, her eyes catching on the paper, reading the few small lines over and over.

Enid ignored her and fetched Guido from his crib. Ainslie's shocked face was the one that greeted the little boy when Enid brought him down.

'I need to go out!'

'Is everything okay?'

'Of course….' Her mind was going at a million miles an hour. Her first instinct had been to just grab her bag and run. Only Elijah's instructions that she keep Guido with her held her back, had her doing up his coat with trembling hands, putting on his hat, clipping him in his stroller and then bumping him down the stairs.

'It's really no trouble for me to watch him. Or I could call Tony for you—he's just on the phone…'

'It will be nice for him to get some air!' Ainslie forced a smile and, knowing Enid was watching from the window, forced herself not to run, chatting away to Guido as she headed for the underground, checking over her shoulder as she hit the high street, frowning as she swiped her Oyster card.

Surely not! Ainslie decided as she plunged into the underground—as if Enid would be following her!

Such flights of fancy flew from her mind the second she emerged at her destination, running now along the familiar street, tears filling her eyes at all he was going through.

And when she saw his tired smile as he opened the door it was entirely natural to fall into his arms and both give and receive a cuddle.

'Oh, Angus,' Ainslie sobbed, 'I just read it in the paper. I only just heard. I'm so sorry for all that you're going through.'

CHAPTER THIRTEEN

'WE'RE fine!' Just as nice, and just as assured as he always had been, for the hundredth time Angus reassured her.

Ainslie was sloshing in tea. His mother, who had flown down from Scotland to help, had made them a vast pot, then taken Guido to play with Jack and Clemmie and left them to get on with it.

'And despite what the papers say it really wasn't a shock. Our marriage has been over for ages.'

'Then why did you stay together?'

'The plan was to keep things going till both the children were at school. We got a nanny so that Gemma could keep her career and I would hopefully make enough money in the meantime, before I ended up a single dad—which isn't an easy thing to be when you're an A&E consultant.'

'And a celebrity doctor.'

'Pays well!' Angus gave a tired grin back. 'I don't want them brought up by nannies.

'I've had help from one of the nurses at the hospital, Imogen—she's Australian like you, and now mum's here—honestly, I've got it all under control.'

'So you really are okay?' Ainslie asked Angus.

'I really am,' Angus confirmed. 'What about you?'

'I'm doing okay.'

'You're welcome here, Ainslie…you know that.'

'That's good to know.' Ainslie smiled as he glanced at his watch and winced.

'Celebrity doctor calls!'

'I'd better go too.'

'Ainslie…' Angus frowned as he saw her to the door and she strapped in Guido. 'When Gemma accused you…'

And she'd never been more grateful for Guido's terrible manners—never been more grateful for a fifteen-month-old throwing a hissy fit as she clipped him in. She didn't really want to tell Angus what had happened that day.

Some things a deserted husband really didn't need to know, no matter how well he was doing, and at that moment Ainslie decided again that no one, not even Angus would ever hear that particular piece of truth from her.

'Elijah!'

He was the last person she'd been expecting to see when she arrived home. And not only was he there, but his smile was wide, his mood buoyant. When they walked in he scooped Guido into his arms, raining his face with kisses before landing a deep one on Ainslie's mouth.

'Where were you?'

'Just walking.' Ainslie shrugged, wondering how she could tell him, or not tell him, and deciding to work that one out later.

'Enid said you rushed off—that you seemed upset.'

'I just needed to think.'

'Me too!' And even though Guido was between them,

suddenly it was just they two. Ainslie a bit shy in the knowledge that she loved him, and Elijah somewhat hesitant too. 'We need to talk,' he said softly.

'I know.'

'Really talk,' he confirmed. 'Because this little guy deserves what's best for him—and we deserve what's best for us as well.'

'I know that too.'

'Not here, though.' Elijah smiled, an easy, natural smile she had never before witnessed, and there was an ease to him that was as confusing as it was welcome.

'Enid?' He turned to the housekeeper as she walked in. 'Would you be able to watch Guido tonight? I want to take Ainslie out for dinner.'

'Of course!' Enid beamed, taking the little guy and leaving them alone.

'I have to go out for an hour,' he said, pulling her grumbling into his arms. 'I know, I know.' He smiled into her hair. 'There's just a couple of things I need to clear up.'

'Like what?'

'I'll tell you over dinner.' He kissed her thoroughly, giving her just a taste of what was to come later, before reluctantly letting her go and opening the front door.

'What?' He registered her frown. 'Ainslie, I really will tell you everything later.'

'It's not that. I just…' She laughed at her own paranoia. 'I feel as if I'm being watched—you haven't got Enid spying on me, have you?'

'Enid?' Elijah grinned as Tony opened the car door. 'No, I haven't got Enid spying on you.'

'Maybe Ms Anderson has.'

'That really is paranoid.' He kissed her again on the lips. 'I'll tell you everything tonight.'

He would.

She just knew.

And so would she.

Would somehow summon the courage to tell him she loved him—loved him so much that she couldn't be a fill-in fiancée or a fill-in wife, could only be the real thing—and if that wasn't what he wanted then she needed to know.

So she readied herself for their first proper date.

She bathed herself in oils and scent, and put on her very favourite knickers—hoping, *hoping* to find out if they were his favourite too. Winced as she sprayed deodorant under newly shaved arms then set to work on hair that was so spectacularly cut now that it just fell into glossy shape.

Her trembling fingers even somehow managed eyeliner, and the thrill in the pit of the stomach grew as she pulled on stockings and shoes and a certain little black dress that had been chosen for her. Her cleavage was spectacularly enhanced by a certain ruby—so much so that she didn't even need earrings, didn't need a single thing except whatever it was Elijah had to say.

Hearing his key in the door, she felt her nerves catch up a touch, causing her to breathe in a few times before dabbing at her lipstick and then heading down the stairs, ready to face her future.

His back was to her, and when he turned around the shy smile on her face faded as she saw his expression.

The loathing, the hatred in his eyes, halted her.

'Judas!' He spat the word, and it hit her like a slap. 'You lying slut.'

And this from the man she'd been about to confess her love to.

'Here!' He mounted the stairs in two long strides. 'Before your brain comes up with an excuse—I'll show you there can *be* no excuse. Walking?' he shouted, thrusting photos into her shaking hands. 'Thinking? You lie so easily you probably don't even know you are doing it.'

And his irrefutable evidence was there for her to see.

The friendly cuddle between herself and Angus sordid and sullied now as she flicked through the photos.

'You *did* have me followed!'

'Of course I had you followed. Did you think I would trust you with my nephew otherwise?'

'Yes…' Ainslie whispered at his hot angry breath. 'Yes—because stupid me actually thought that you did.'

'Did what?' he roared, as Enid came out to see what all the noise was about. Tony followed behind—his services seemingly not now required for tonight.

'Trust me.' Ainslie shuddered the words out. 'Somehow, in all of this, I believed that somewhere deep down you trusted me, and somehow—despite my head telling me otherwise—somehow I trusted you too.' Handing back the photos, she didn't offer any defence—didn't need to make excuses for herself to him. 'Clearly I was wrong—on both counts.'

'And that's it?' Elijah demanded. 'That is all you have to say for yourself?'

'That's it.' Ainslie nodded, sniffing back her tears and somehow standing proud.

'Tony?' She called to his driver. She couldn't even face going up the stairs to get her things, couldn't stand to be in his presence a second longer. 'Can you take me to a hotel, please? Enid…' She forced a smile at her lovely friend. 'I shan't be needing the spare room tonight.'

'Ainslie…' Elijah grabbed her wrist as she headed for the door, but she shook him off.

'I'm running, Elijah, but I'm not hiding. Tony will tell you where I'm staying, and just as soon as you send my things on I'll check out. Oh, and I'd hurry if I were you,' she added. 'You know how much I like nice things!'

And that was almost all she had to say for herself—she swore that from this day on she'd never defend herself to him.

'*You're* the Judas.' Ainslie called out as her parting shot.

So the charade they'd started continued.

No draughty hostel or serviced apartment for Elijah Vanaldi's ex-fiancée.

The plushest of London hotels, a famous name in her guidebook, was suddenly home for now.

Nothing was too much trouble when she arrived in the vast lobby in her little black dress, with a tissue sodden with tears.

A luxury suite was arranged in a trice.

Strawberry daiquiris and white chocolate ice cream with hot raspberry sauce was sent up on her endless demand.

She'd never wanted his money—Ainslie knew that—but she'd damn well spend it. Would stoop to his gutter level because he expected nothing less.

But it didn't help.

Nothing helped.

Nothing dimmed her pain.

Not the ninety-minute massage or the pampering facial. Not the wardrobe that had materialised as if by magic, thanks to the personal shopper the concierge, without a turn of his hair, had discreetly arranged.

And she wished he'd stop her credit card—wished, *wished* he'd send her her things. Ainslie sobbed into her very soft pillow and wished, *wished* that this horrible bit was over, so that somehow she could move on. So that somehow she could pick up the pieces and salvage what was left of her heart.

Only it couldn't last—the frenzied spending, the venom, the hate. It just wasn't her—the gold-digging woman she'd played for a night and a day was so far removed from the red swollen face that looked back at her from the mirror it made her wince.

'Enough!' she told her reflection—because it was.

She didn't need to wait for the master to send her things—didn't need to explain herself to him.

And it would have been nice to keep it, but it would surely hurt for ever to look at so she took off her necklace and placed it in an envelope with her note.

Handed it in to Reception as she settled her bill.

'Could you make sure that Elijah Vanaldi gets this when he contacts the hotel?'

'Of course.'

'It should probably go in the safe,' Ainslie added, turning around. That funny old feeling was back now, and she was sure, quite sure, she was being watched.

She probably was, Ainslie decided, slipping the receipt into her purse.

Clearly Elijah liked to keep an eye on his *things*.

Well, she wasn't one of his things any more. So, to the receptionist's discreet cough, Ainslie turned around and stuck up two fingers for the camera, deciding to have afternoon tea while she was there!

Only this bill she would settle herself.

CHAPTER FOURTEEN

COULD he forgive her?

Elijah asked the unthinkable for the thousandth time.

The house was a morgue without her.

The Christmas tree had been taken down, the decorations packed away, and just this vast empty void remained in his soul where the grieving must now begin. For all *he* had lost, for all Guido had lost too.

'Ijah!' A delicious smile dragged him from the depths, a face full of dribbles and an endless supply of wet kisses stared up from his knees, banana-smeared hands reaching out for a cuddle. *'Ijah.'*

'So you learn my name?' Scooping him up, Elijah gazed at him, stared into eyes that were like mirrors, and the answers he'd sought so hard to find were there for him to see.

His search had brought up nothing, his hunch had proved unfounded. He had found nothing to pin the Castellas with Maria's and Rico's death. Now, with Ainslie gone, when Ms Anderson found out—as she surely would—that it had all been a ruse, Social Services' decision would be inevitable. Elijah had conceded his playboy, jet-setting lifestyle really wasn't fitting for a small child, so, yes, maybe Guido *would* be better off with two parents and cousins. Even if to Elijah they weren't ideal.

There was just one detail he hadn't factored in when he'd been searching his soul to make the best choices for his nephew's future. One slight hiccough in all his mental calculations that Elijah hadn't spotted.

'I love you.'

For the first time in his life Elijah said it, and it was like opening the lid on a shaken bottle. Bubbles fizzed in, and he felt the utter release that came with such a simple truth.

'I do.' He smiled at his nephew, smiled because Guido neither noticed nor cared how monumental this moment was. 'Which means I'm going to have to keep you.'

'Ijah!' Guido chanted, maybe not so oblivious after all.

'Which may not please some people…' Elijah gave a grim smile. But he was ready for the challenge now—there wasn't a fight he couldn't win if he didn't put his heart into it.

Except one.

'What do I do?'

Again he asked Guido, and again Guido didn't answer.

'Hey…' Elijah kissed his soggy face. 'At least I'll get the sympathy vote from the single mothers at the play place you go to…'

'Playgroup…' Enid said, walking in unheard. 'My sister just called. I was hoping to meet her for coffee—I thought I might take Guido.' Enid's voice was polite and formal, just as it had been since Ainslie had left, but he could feel her holding back, knew there was plenty she'd like to say to him—that he was a fool, an idiot, that he'd let the best thing that had ever happened to him walk out of the door. But Enid didn't have to say it.

Elijah knew it already.

'I suppose you'll be discussing us?'

'No,' Enid replied coolly. 'As I said, I'm having coffee with my sister. But she did say that she wanted to come back here and speak with you after.'

'Fine,' Elijah snapped, then relented—after all, none of this was her fault. 'Tony can drive you,' he offered, though privately he was glad of the excuse to be alone—really alone—with his grief. 'Feel free to tell her I'm not giving up on Guido.'

'Glad to hear it.' Enid's face softened. 'But it would be easier with Ainslie.'

'It would…' Elijah conceded. 'And a whole lot nicer too—but we'll be okay…' He ruffled Guido's hair. 'The two of us will make it work.'

Enid took Guido off to get him ready, which left Elijah alone with his thoughts—and for the hundredth time he berated himself for his haste to accuse rather than to listen. Maybe she'd just gone to say goodbye to Angus? Elijah wondered hopelessly as he logged onto his computer. One final time together for old times' sake? Hell, he'd done that on many occasions himself—why shouldn't the same rules apply to her?

They just didn't.

And they didn't apply to him any more either.

Picking up the little black box by the computer, he opened it, stared at the mocking ring.

He'd being going to ask her.

Properly.

Ahead of the Social Services decision. Because that had seemed important somehow.

On his flight home Elijah had realised that though the decision was vital to him, to *them* it didn't actually matter. He needed her for so much more than Guido.

Needed that loyal, feisty, funny, beautiful woman in every aspect of his life.

A woman who could even make him smile now, when he tracked her manic spending.

In the hours she'd been gone she'd done pretty well, but his smile faded when he realised that she must have checked out.

Somewhere deep inside he'd known that she would.

He was scanning the entries now—for a sum so little it shouldn't matter. The fact it wasn't there actually mattered a lot, brought tears to dry eyes. He realised she'd paid for his Christmas present herself. But again, somewhere deep inside he'd already known that she had.

But men couldn't be seen crying.

Especially when Enid informed him that she was on her way out and that his nemesis was at the front door.

'Should I show Dr Maitlin in?'

'No—I'll see him at the door.'

'It's not doing much good there…' For the first time Enid interfered, glancing down to the ring he was holding. 'Sitting in a box when it should be on her finger.'

'I'll tell her that, shall I?' Elijah's sarcasm didn't faze Enid. 'When I see her next?'

'Happen you should!'

Clearing his throat, Elijah stood, unclenched his fists, and vowed to himself that he wouldn't hit him, would only open the door. It was a promise he wasn't sure he could keep.

'Is Ainslie in?'

It took a supreme effort to tell him where she was staying—but the barb on his tongue still needed an out.

'You'd better hurry, though—it would seem she just checked out—or checked in with the next rich fool to come along.'

'Sorry?' Angus frowned. 'I was asking after Ainslie. I just wanted to clear something up.'

'Well, she's gone.'

'Fine…' Angus turned to go, and then changed his mind. 'If she does get in touch, would you ask her to call me?'

Elijah's fists balled at his sides. New Year's resolutions were fading fast and he was sorely tempted to knock his lights out.

'Only I think I owe her an apology.'

'*Aspetta*! Wait!' Elijah instructed, watching Angus's shoulders stiffen. Clearly he was a man not used to being told! 'Look…' Elijah closed his eyes and struggled to keep his voice even, because even if he might not like what he was about to hear he badly needed to hear it. 'Would you mind coming inside? Would you mind explaining what is going on with you and Ainslie?'

'Let's just leave it.' Angus was walking away.

'I read your reference for her…' Elijah gave a tight smile. 'I was hoping to clarify a couple of points—perhaps I should ring your wife?'

'You'd have to find her first.' Reluctantly Angus came in and sat down in the study. 'My marriage has just broken up, so believe me—I'm not in the mood for small talk.'

'Me neither.' Elijah gave a tight smile. 'Ainslie told me when I hired her that she was fired because she had been accused of theft.' He knew it was a white lie, but he needed to find out exactly what was going on here.

'She told you about it?' Angus frowned. 'And you still employed her?'

'Ainslie wouldn't steal.' Without hesitation he said it. He believed in her then just as he had on that day—and with that came the appalling realisation that she wouldn't cheat either. That the suspicious, mistrusting world he had inhabited all his life had blinded him to simple beauty. 'Ainslie would not have stolen your wife's necklace. I know that.'

'I wish I had!' Angus let out a long sigh. 'Look—I have no desire to give you the details, but at the time it didn't sit right with me, and I told Ainslie that. She came to see me yesterday—when she read in the paper that my marriage had ended—and unfortunately it never entered my head to ask her till she was leaving… She was too busy checking that the kids and I were okay. And then it dawned on me—she didn't steal that necklace; that would have been my wife's excuse to get rid of her. I wondered if perhaps Ainslie had found out that my wife was having an affair.'

'Was she?'

'Oh, yes!' Angus gave a wry laugh. 'All I asked from my sham of a marriage was that we were faithful—something it would appear my ex-wife couldn't adhere to.'

'And you did?'

'Absolutely.'

And the strength, the unwavering conviction in his voice, suddenly had Elijah feeling very small—very small indeed.

'I am going to see Ainslie now—hoping to see her,' Elijah added. 'If I do, I will pass on what you have said.'

'Thank you.' Angus shook his hand. 'And I'm sorry about your family.'

'She told you about my sister?'

'Ainslie wouldn't discuss anything like that. I spoke to you on the phone. The day of the accident.'

'It was you?' Elijah's face paled, recalling again the awful call that had changed his life in so many ways.

'I was the receiving doctor when your sister was brought in. I'm very sorry for your loss.'

'Thank you.' It was all he could manage. All he could manage as he was plunged from hell to hell—remembering Angus's kindness that day, the voice on the phone that had gently delivered the hardest of news, remembering again, living again, what had happened to his family, the fear that had gripped him until Ainslie had come along.

Until she'd waltzed into his life and somehow made it bearable.

Because without her he truly didn't know how he'd have coped.

'One other thing….' Angus cleared his throat, paused for the longest time before speaking again.

Elijah could never have guessed the indecision behind the strong voice—could never have guessed that what was about to be delivered was absolutely against Angus's usually impeccable better judgement. Angus could almost see his medical licence flashing before a BMA review panel, but somehow it seemed imperative to go on.

'You'll no doubt hear soon anyway—though I'd prefer that you didn't mention you've heard it from me…'

'Hear what?' Elijah's hackles were raised, the intuition, the gut instinct that had led him from the streets to a penthouse, telling him that this was big.

'A detective contacted me this afternoon… It would appear your sister and brother-in-law's case is being reopened—it would seem it's not quite as open and shut as it first appeared.' He gave an uncomfortable shrug. 'Just so you know.'

He *had* known.

From the minute he'd seen his sister at some level he'd known. But at every turn he'd been thwarted, called irrational, tired, paranoid. Yet he'd known that it had been no accident—and now it would seem he was about to be proved right.

Without her!

The words buzzed in his ears—his throat was impossibly dry as he tried to speak. 'Who was the detective you spoke with?'

'I'd rather not say. Wait till they contact you.' Angus was heading down the steps now, walking out onto the street. He jumped a touch as Elijah grabbed his shoulder, spinning him around. As a trauma doctor Angus knew what he was seeing, witnessed naked fear in Elijah eyes.

'I need to know!' he shouted, and Angus knew it wasn't at him. 'I think Ainslie is in danger.'

The detective wasn't so easily convinced.

Elijah—wanting to shoot from the hip, wanting only to go to her—paced the lounge like a caged lion as the detective insisted on details.

'You hired private detectives,' he pointed out. 'That explains why she thought she was being followed.'

'It does…' Elijah said through gritted teeth. 'And I hired a bodyguard for Guido. Initially I was worried the Castellas might try to take him, and when I became suspicious I hired a private detective. Your colleagues,' he added, with more than a dash of resentment, 'didn't take my concerns seriously when I rang them after I spoke with the social worker.'

'Maybe they did,' the detective replied. 'Given that the case is being re-examined.'

'I always thought that Rico's family might be behind this—from the moment I realised they knew this house was in Maria's and Rico's names I was sure it had to be more than a coincidence. So I went to Italy to check up on them.'

'Hoping to find what?'

'Something—anything. I wanted to see if they'd paid a deposit for the apartment they're living in now—if they'd paid out any large sums.'

'You accessed their bank accounts?'

Elijah nodded without guilt—because he hadn't a shred—just as he hadn't had a shred of guilt when he'd called in a favour at the New Year's Eve party. 'I had to go there—they wouldn't give me any information over the phone.'

'And had they?'

'No.' The detective opened his mouth to speak, then thought better of it. But Elijah answered for him. 'Their financial situation is dire.'

'That's not a crime,' the detective said. 'And neither is stopping to purchase a gift at the airport. If you thought there was danger—why did you leave?'

'Because I had to find out what was going on. I had my nephew moved to the fourth floor. I had a bodyguard posing as my driver, watching Guido all the time, and I had a private detective parked outside the house to keep an eye on Ainslie.'

'Where is the private detective now?'

'I called him off—I thought they were safe,' Elijah roared. 'I thought for once I was wrong, that I was just being paranoid. But Ainslie thought she was being watched again yesterday.' Elijah stared the detective straight in the eye.

'And was she?'

'Not by my detective—I was on my way to meet him.'

'You believe she's in imminent danger?'

Elijah nodded, and it was Angus pacing now—Angus who greeted an utterly bemused Enid and Ms Anderson when they walked in.

'Find Ainslie!' Elijah called to Tony, before he was even through the door, his voice nearing desperation as he tried to spell out to the detective just how dire things really were. 'They think we are still engaged. They have no reason to think otherwise. Without Ainslie—' he gulped in air as he said it. 'Without Ainslie I would not be granted custody of my nephew.'

'You know that for sure?'

'I think I was about to find out.' Elijah glanced over to Ms Anderson, who nodded.

'But the Castellas wouldn't know that—' the detective pointed out.

'The Castella family know,' Ms Anderson interrupted. 'I just informed them of them of my decision. That in my opinion, for now at least, Guido should stay where he is— with Elijah and his fiancée.'

'Stay put.' The detective was pulling out his phone. 'I'll get a uniformed officer to stay with you. Don't go getting any big ideas…' He waited till the two men obediently sat before racing out through the door. But the second his car skidded off Elijah looked over to Angus.

Elijah was already standing. 'He *is* joking—he doesn't just expect us to sit here?'

He knew how the Castellas worked. Had grown up on rough streets himself. The instinct that had got him through his childhood and teenage years had taught him a thing or three, and not to use that now—to leave Ainslie to the Castellas—was incomprehensible.

And if they harmed her—if they hurt her—if because of his actions, the world carried on without her…

Elijah closed his eyes as Angus sped off.

It was unthinkable.

CHAPTER FIFTEEN

SHE felt better—well, how could she not?

She had feasted on the tiniest of sandwiches, each delectable crustless finger a taste sensation, and on the most divine raisin and apple scones, smeared with strawberry jam and clotted cream, and tiny little pastries served on a three-tiered silver server—all for her! And the surroundings were to die for! Her mind was soothed by the music that wafted in the air around her, and with a glass of champagne in her hand, endless aromatic tea waiting to be sipped, it was hard not to believe that life wouldn't again be good.

Afternoon tea, she'd found out, usually had to be booked weeks in advance, but given she'd been a paying guest—well, she'd been shown right through. Had sat and people-watched and realised, with a very brave smile, that she was lucky to be here.

Lucky to sample a taste of a life that was so far removed from hers.

Lucky to have had him—even if just for a little while.

And as Ainslie stepped out onto the street, walked out under the arches and felt the late-afternoon sun on her face, heading where she didn't quite know, but would soon work out, Ainslie also knew that, whatever he chose to believe, Elijah had been lucky to have her.

She could ring Angus, Ainslie mused. Or then again perhaps not. She wasn't really up to being around anyone, wanted to be alone a little while longer to lick her wounds...

'Sorry!' So deep was she in her thoughts, Ainslie actually thought she had bumped into someone. It took a second for her to realise that this was no accident. Her bag was being tugged from her shoulder.

Her first instinct was to cling on, to scream for help— only she was mute, stepping into survival mode and knowing she should just let it go. A bag wasn't worth fighting over—so she didn't. She just let the strap slip down her arm, her heart pumping, wanting the man gone. Only it didn't happen. She could see her bag being tossed on the ground, and Ainslie glimpsed real fear for the first time in her life as everything seemed to move in slow motion—the stench of body odour hit her, the wail of sirens was growing louder and louder, and she had the horrible, horrible realisation that he had a knife. This man who had taken her bag had a knife—and he was going to use it.

She'd never expected to wake up to him again.

Had said goodbye to that dream already.

But maybe she *was* dreaming—because it didn't actually look like Elijah. The Elijah she knew didn't cry, and this one had been.

'He stabbed me.' It was the second thought that came into her head, and her hands raced to her body, trying to locate her pain.

'No!' He moved to soothe her, but he couldn't. She

could feel the needle of the drip in her arm, could see her blood on his shirt, could remember the knife.

'Oh, God!' Panic was building. 'What will I tell my mum?'

'That you didn't get stabbed.' He lifted up his shirt, showed her a very white dressing against a very nice stomach, and on his tired grey face he managed a smile. 'That was me. You fainted when you saw that I had been stabbed, and hit your head on the pavement.'

'You?' It didn't make sense, but it was starting to, like trying to remember a dream. Little fragments of images pierced her mind—a wedge of muscle against her, the pungent scent of her assailant overridden by a beautiful, familiar, masculine smell, and then drenching her the sweet, heady relief that Elijah was here, that she would be safe, that he would make everything right. 'How did you know to be there…?' Her head thrashed on the pillow in confusion. 'Were you having me followed again?'

'No…but I wish to God I had been though. Ainslie, I had you followed while I was away because I feared for you—and feared for Guido too.'

'Feared for us?'

'It wasn't an accident that killed my sister and Rico— it was a hit. Marco and Dina arranged to have them killed.' He held her hands tighter as he admitted what he'd exposed her to, and she knew it wasn't paranoia or hate that was speaking, knew she was hearing the truth. 'And yours was not a random mugging—though that was how it was supposed to appear. A mugging that got out of hand…' He actually flinched as he said it. 'You were supposed to be killed too.'

'Me?'

'You,' Elijah confirmed. 'Because without you I would never have been granted custody of Guido.'

She felt sick, actually physically sick, at the thought someone would want her dead—that someone, anyone, could care so much for money and so little for life.

He needed a shave. Funny the things you thought about. Funny that something so irrelevant should come into her focus as everything changed. But he really *did* need a shave—the designer stubble he'd worn yesterday was far heavier now. He looked like a gypsy, Ainslie decided, as he took her hand, and tears filled her eyes for what Guido would one day have to hear.

'The police have arrested and charged them….' Closing his eyes, he brought a hand to his chin, index finger pressed against his lips, dragging air in and out for a minute as he tried to find the formula to an unknown poison. 'I had my suspicions—suddenly they'd found out Maria and Rico had money…to me it seemed too much of a coincidence—but then I told myself I was being ridiculous, that they would never want them dead. The police at the time seemed confident it was an accident. And Ms Anderson—everyone—seemed to think it reasonable that, despite the differences between the families, they would want to take care of their orphaned nephew…'

She looked at him with new eyes now. The man who had to her seemed so bitter and mistrusting had been—but for all the right reasons.

'Tony isn't my driver—he's a bodyguard. I hired him to keep an eye on Guido. At first I thought they might try to take him, but then the more I thought about it the more I was convinced they were to do with the accident.'

'That's why you had Guido moved to the top floor?' A frown creased her brow.

'Tony watched the house at night.'

A smile that was utterly out of place shone for a second as she saw things differently. 'That's why he never gave you a lift?'

'Unless I was with Guido.' Elijah nodded. 'The fact that they stopped to buy a present at the airport…'

That long-ago bedroom conversation came back to her mind, his sheer bewilderment at their actions, which had revealed the depths of the pain he must feel.

'I couldn't fathom that, Ainslie. I vomited at the airport—I had to face the same as them—I could not have thought to buy a gift. I didn't go to Italy to break up with Portia. I had already taken care of that. I went to Italy to check things out. I broke into their home, looked through their things—that New Year party we went to was about chatting up an old friend who had a contact that worked in their bank, I couldn't do it over the phone—I had to go there to view their accounts. And, yes, they were poor, but there was nothing to indicate they intended to travel—nothing in their home that confirmed my doubts—so I let it go. I told myself I was being stupid. I arrived back in London and I rang the private detective I had hired to watch over you and Guido—he had nothing on them either, so I called him off. I was about to call Tony off too—and that was when the private detective asked to meet with me—he said it was nothing to do with the Castellas, but he had some photos that I might want to see.'

'Angus and I?'

He nodded. 'Angus came to see me this afternoon—

amongst other things he told me that the police had contacted him. Forensics had come back on the car, and it appeared someone had tampered with the fuel tank. It looked like a professional job—someone who knew what they were doing. Given the ferocity of the fire, it was lucky it was picked up. They got rid of Maria and Rico and they tried to get rid of you.'

'Why?' The most pointless of questions, because there could never be a right answer. 'For money?'

'It wasn't just about money—though that would have been their first motive. It was about hatred, about revenge… All I know is that they couldn't even wait—they wiped their nephew's parents off the face of the earth just to get their hands on his money and just to get back at Maria for being a part of me.' He stared down at her bemused face as she struggled to comprehend such atrocities, struggled to accept the world in which he'd grown up—*this*—Elijah berated himself over and over—the woman he had refused to trust. 'That is what hate does to you.'

'And that's why you're going to have to somehow learn to forgive them…' She smiled at his incredulous face, but he closed his mouth when she spoke on. 'For Guido's sake—or he's going to grow up filled with hatred too. Elijah—why didn't you tell me?'

'How?' he asked. 'How could I tell you my suspicions and expect you to stay? All I could do was protect you—at first it was for Guido—and then…' Even now he couldn't fully tell her of the fear that had gripped him, of the paranoia that had convinced him everything he loved was in danger of being taken. 'I needed you to stay, but I wanted you to leave.'

'You should have told me.'

'I tried to.'

She closed her eyes in regret—because he had.

'We were fighting for the same thing from different corners,' Elijah said softly. 'You could only see good, whereas I...'

'It would have been nice to meet in the middle.'

'I am going to speak with Ms Anderson.' He swallowed hard. 'I have to do what is best for Guido and she is right—my lifestyle is not suited to a small child, not suited to any child...'

And she couldn't bear it—couldn't bear the thought of little Guido being a number in the system. Surely whatever love Elijah could offer was better than that? And then she halted. Because it wasn't—wasn't good enough for Guido the same way it wasn't good enough for her.

'You have to do what you think is right.' Her voice was strained. 'You will see him, though?' Ainslie checked. 'You will ring and keep in touch...?'

'I'll see him every day!' Elijah frowned. 'Are you feeling all right? Is your head hurting?' And then he got it. 'He's mine,' Elijah said simply. 'I don't have to prove that to Ms Anderson and I don't have to prove it to myself—now I know it in my heart. I am going to move here. I don't want to unsettle him again. He needs to have the people and the things he loves around him for a while. Enid is good for him, and Tony is looking to retire, so maybe he would work for me too—as a driver this time...'

'What about your work?' Ainslie asked. 'What about the travel and the parties and the women...?'

'Everything in moderation,' Elijah answered. 'Especially the women.' His eyes held hers. 'I'm hoping to scale them right back, actually—down to one!'

'It's not that straightforward.'

'I don't want to be without you,' Elijah interrupted. 'Never, ever again.'

'Because of Guido?'

'Because of *you*.'

Which was the right answer. But still she pulled her hands away—because even if it was extreme, the hate that had led them to this point was an extension of themselves. He was so mistrusting, so unsure. She remembered again the hell he'd put her through—remembered again every hurt.

'I never slept with Angus.'

'I know that.'

'But you *didn't* know that,' Ainslie countered. 'Which means that you don't know me.'

'I do now.'

'Which is too late.' It was the hardest thing to do, to turn her back on a future she so badly wanted—but as much as she loved him, she loved herself more. 'Now I've passed all the tests suddenly you decide that I'm good enough? Well, guess what? I always was.'

'What was I supposed to think?'

'You didn't think; you just assumed—saw a photo…'

'I'm not talking about the photos!' Irritated, annoyed, the old Elijah was back, his bedside manner fading as he stood up and paced the room. 'I walk out of that hospital and on to the underground, holding my nephew, and I pray to God, to the universe, to anyone listening, for help—for something to happen, to show me the way. And I open my eyes and there *you* are.' He jabbed a finger accusingly.

'Everything okay?' A nurse popped her head in and frowned.

'Everything's fine,' Elijah snapped, and Ainslie nodded.

But the second they were alone, she rounded on him, furious, *furious*, that he thought he could talk to her like that—furious that she was lying in a hospital bed and being told off. She told him so!

'I was nearly stabbed this afternoon!'

'I *was* stabbed this afternoon!' Elijah countered.

'I've been mugged, attacked…'

'Scoffing down afternoon tea?' Elijah hurled just in case she was expecting sympathy. 'Booking massages and personal shoppers?'

'You can't talk to me like that.'

'So I'm supposed to just walk out?' He glared. 'Let you turn your back on the best thing that will ever happen to you? Because I'm telling you now—' his voice rose as she opened her mouth to argue '—no one will ever love you as much as I do.'

And he meant it.

Because only Elijah could shout it the first time he said it.

'I loved you even when I thought the worst—hell, Ainslie, I spent this morning wondering if I was mad because I was ready to forgive you for sleeping with a married man. I told myself that despite everything I believe in, every standard I'd set for the woman who would be my wife, that if it really was just one last time it would be better to forgive you than to lose you.'

It had never entered her head that his love might be greater than hers—that Elijah might forgive something she never, ever could.

'It was so much easier to doubt you than to believe in you.'

'Why?' She just didn't get it—honestly couldn't fathom why he had chosen, at every turn, to think the worst.

Till he told her.

Walking over, he sat on the bed and word for word he said it again—only softly this time, holding her hands instead of jabbing a finger. 'I walk out of that hospital and on to the underground, holding my nephew, and I pray to God, to the universe, to anyone listening, for help—for something to happen, to show me the way. And I open my eyes and there you are. *You!*' he added. 'The only person who didn't walk on, the only person who stopped. Who came back with me to a house I was dreading entering, who took care of my nephew. And who fell in love with me.'

She nodded—not embarrassed, not blushing—just nodded at the simple truth. Tears streamed down her cheeks as he struggled to explain what had taken place in that beautiful head of his.

'It was easier to think of you as a mistress, a gold-digger...'

'Easier?' Ainslie frowned. 'How could that be easier?'

'Prayers don't just get answered. You don't give out your wishes and expect an instant response. You don't just open your eyes and the woman you've always wanted is there. Miracles don't just happen.'

'But they do,' Ainslie countered.

Love—the miracle that occurred over the globe, thousands upon thousands of times every day. Random people the world over were looking up to find their soul mate looking back at them—the person, whether they realised it or not, who was the very one they were meant to be with.

'Especially at Christmas!' Ainslie said, as if it were obvious. 'Everyone knows that.'

Lifting up her hand and capturing his proud cheek, she looked back with love at the man who had rescued her too that night, who had rescued her again today, and who would, she knew beyond a doubt, rescue her any time she needed it.

'And I guess someone decided that we both deserved a miracle.'

EPILOGUE

HE LOOKED divine.

If she lived to be a hundred then the next seventy-two years, Ainslie realised, clutching her flowers, were going to be spent catching her breath.

Catching her breath at a man who really did stand a head above the rest.

Resplendent in a suit, and somehow holding onto the hand of a very spoilt and thoroughly over-excited Guido, who insisted on being the centre of attention, Elijah was the centre of hers. Even when Guido pulled out his corsage and stamped on it as heads turned to the arriving bride. Even when Guido spat in frustration when the best uncle in the world took the arm of the bride and walked up the aisle.

Ainslie followed behind.

'Do you really think it appropriate that she's wearing white?' he whispered into her ear later, the giver-away of the bride dancing with the bridesmaid.

'Absolutely.' Ainslie nodded dreamily, lifting her head from the haven of his chest to see Enid smiling shyly at Tony.

'What was that?' In a room of couples dancing, he stopped.

'A kick.'

'He kicked!' His hand moved to her velvet-clad belly—held the swell of their baby in his hot palm. He grinned. 'He kicked again! He'll play for Italia!'

'So might *she*!' Ainslie said pointedly.

'Good.' Elijah shrugged. 'Ms Anderson can coach her.'

And even on a thimble of champagne to toast the bride, and a gallon of sparkling water and orange juice, he made her drunk with laughter. Reprobate, irrepressible, yet somehow incredibly tender—Elijah: the miracle that just kept giving.

'Guido is going to be so jealous when the baby comes...' Elijah sighed into her hair.

'He's already jealous.' Ainslie grinned, watching as he pummelled the floor with his fists as Ainslie's mother, who was over for Christmas, tried to soothe him. 'Fancy us two having the nerve to dance and forget to ask him!'

'He's getting better, though?' Elijah checked, and she nodded.

It had been hard, because despite his tender age Guido had missed his parents—still missed them, Ainslie was sure—but they were doing their best to fill that gap.

'He's getting there.'

And so were they.

Their decision to stay in London had been hard, but the right one. His home was the one constant they could offer Guido when everything else in his little world had shifted. All their worlds had shifted—as the adoption had gone through, as Elijah had scaled back his work, as new relatives had visited from Australia. As *Ijah* slowly became Dad and, one recent day, Ainslie for the first time became Mum.

Yet they helped him remember—the digital photo frame
Ainslie had so lovingly purchased often a source of comfort
for the little boy who did actually miss his parents. Slowly
Guido's house had become their home—and never more so
than now. The tree was back in the lounge, a wreath was
on the door just as it had been last year, parcels were hidden
in the wardrobe, and the house was filled with all the
laughter and tears that came with any family at Christmas—
especially when the mother-in-law comes to stay!

'I love you!' Ainslie said, just in case he needed reminding.

'How could you not?'

It was Elijah who couldn't accept the compliment—
Elijah who made a brave joke and a stab at humour. Elijah
who woke her at night sometimes just to check that she was
there, that this woman who had dashed into his life wasn't
going to disappear in a puff of smoke, just as everyone he
had ever loved before her had. 'You know I love you…'

He stared into her heart and beyond it, took her with that
look to places they would one day visit, to two lifetimes
that were now one and would share together each day.

'I do know,' Ainslie answered, because she did. 'But tell
me again why?'

'Because,' Elijah said, struggling for a moment before
succinctly delivering her the perfect answer. 'Just because…'

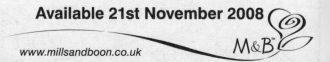

Will sleigh bells turn to wedding bells?

Three gorgeous, glittering Christmas romances featuring:

Silent Night Man by Diana Palmer

Christmas Reunion by Catherine George

A Mistletoe Masquerade by Louise Allen

Available 17th October 2008

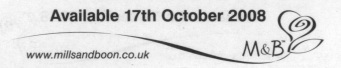

www.millsandboon.co.uk

M&B

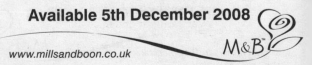

Celebrate 100 years of pure reading pleasure with Mills & Boon®

To mark our centenary, each month we're publishing a special 100th Birthday Edition. These celebratory editions are packed with extra features and include a FREE bonus story.

Plus, you have the chance to enter a fabulous monthly prize draw. See 100th Birthday Edition books for details.

Now that's worth celebrating!

September 2008

Crazy about her Spanish Boss by Rebecca Winters
Includes FREE bonus story
Rafael's Convenient Proposal

November 2008

**The Rancher's Christmas Baby
by Cathy Gillen Thacker**
Includes FREE bonus story *Baby's First Christmas*

December 2008

One Magical Christmas by Carol Marinelli
Includes FREE bonus story *Emergency at Bayside*

Look for Mills & Boon® 100th Birthday Editions at your favourite bookseller or visit
www.millsandboon.co.uk

FREE

4 BOOKS AND A SURPRISE GIFT!

We would like to take this opportunity to thank you for reading this Mills & Boon® book by offering you the chance to take FOUR more specially selected titles from the Modern™ series absolutely FREE! We're also making this offer to introduce you to the benefits of the Mills & Boon® Book Club—

- ★ **FREE home delivery**
- ★ **FREE gifts and competitions**
- ★ **FREE monthly Newsletter**
- ★ **Books available before they're in the shops**
- ★ **Exclusive Mills & Boon® Book Club offers**

Accepting these FREE books and gift places you under no obligation to buy; you may cancel at any time, even after receiving your free shipment. Simply complete your details below and return the entire page to the address below. You don't even need a stamp!

YES! Please send me 4 free Modern books and a surprise gift. I understand that unless you hear from me, I will receive 6 superb new titles every month for just £2.99 each, postage and packing free. I am under no obligation to purchase any books and may cancel my subscription at any time. The free books and gift will be mine to keep in any case.

P8ZEE

Ms/Mrs/Miss/Mr..Initials ....

BLOCK CAPITALS PLEASE

Surname ....

Address ....

....

....Postcode ....

Send this whole page to:

The Mills & Boon Book Club, FREEPOST CN81, Croydon, CR9 3WZ